I0673705

LIFE OF LOVE

Santonu Kumar Dhar

Shobha Publishing

In accordance with the U.S. Copyright Act of 1976, no part of this publication may be reproduced, distributed, or transmitted in any form or by any means, or stored in a database or retrieval system, without the prior written permission of the publisher.

Shobha Publishing

Library of Congress Catalogue-in-Publication Data

ISBN-10 : 0615718256
ISBN-13 : 978-0615718255

To my beloved wife

CONTENTS

Life of Love

CHAPTER 1   1

CHAPTER 2   17

CHAPTER 3   31

CHAPTER 4   47

CHAPTER 5   59

CHAPTER 6   72

CHAPTER 7   85

CHAPTER 8   97

CHAPTER 9   110

CHAPTER 10   124

CHAPTER 11   137

CHAPTER 12   148

CHAPTER 13   160

CHAPTER 14   171

CHAPTER 15   183

CHAPTER 16   194

CHAPTER 17   206
CHAPTER 18   217
Acknowledgement   229
About The Author   231

CHAPTER 1

He first saw her at the bus stop. One could say it was love at first sight, but she didn't quite notice him in return. She was absorbed in a magazine, her legs crossed daintily beneath an embroidered silk dress. Her auburn hair fell in waves around her shoulders and her bright, emerald-green eyes were alive with delight. She was beautiful beyond comparison, so much that he made a move to sit next to her.

John Deane was a handsome, clean-shaven, 27-year-old software engineer. He graduated in computer science at Harvard University and now co-owned a software company with his best friend, Michael Rawl. Michael was to be married that very day, and John was on his way to purchase flowers as a gift. However, his task was no longer at the forefront of his mind. He was fixated on the woman reading the magazine at the bus stop.

He brushed a hand through his dark hair, feeling a little self-conscious that he was already losing it along the sides of his head. He blamed it on the stress of his job.

Just as he took a step towards the bench, another man of about thirty slipped in front of him and touched the woman's shoulder.

"Sarah?"

She looked up from her magazine and saw the tall man greeting her, and then stood gracefully with the loveliest smile John had ever seen. As she stood, she let the magazine fall onto the bench.

"How are you?" he asked.

"William Burnham, is that you?" She opened her arms for a brief hug and a kiss on the cheek, and then stepped back. "I'm well. What are you doing here?"

"I was on my way to meet a client and I just happened to see you sitting over here."

"Well, how nice of you to come and say hello!"

As they chatted to one another of their day and events that had happened since they last spoke, John meandered over to the bench and picked up the magazine. He was curious to know what she was reading, what interested her. On the corner of the magazine, over a stamped sticker addressed to her, he learned her name was Sarah Jane Miller.

Her name rang in his head like a beautiful string of notes, clear and soft as bells. He had never felt such a pull before – such a desire to know a complete stranger.

Then, as if it were a serendipitous sign from

heaven, his ear caught the tail end of Sarah's conversation with William.

"Where are you headed?" he asked.

Ahead of them, the city bus pulled up to the stop, its brakes creaking. Sarah gestured to the machine. "I'm on my way to my cousin Amanda's wedding."

"Oh, how lovely," William replied.

John could barely listen further. His brain was buzzing with excitement; the inertia of thoughts was unstoppable. He was so distracted by his stroke of luck that he watched Sarah board the bus without stopping her to hand over the magazine. The doors were already closed by the time he realized his mistake. He held it up to the bus window, but Sarah wasn't looking out. It didn't matter, though. He had a feeling he would see her again.

He, too, was headed to a wedding later. His friend and business partner, Michael, had shared everything with him since their university days. There were no secrets, between all their great memories together and all

their aspirations.

Michael had started dating a charming girl six months ago, and it was nice for John to see him finally tie the knot with someone. Of course, John had met her a while back and given his "thumbs-up" approval. Her name, just as Sarah had stated moments before, was Amanda.

* * *

Amanda Miller's house was an old Victorian style with beautiful brickwork and low ceilings. The wedding decorations were up, strewn with lights and flowers. It had taken Sarah Jane Miller a long bus ride and several transfers to get from Manhattan to Montclair, New Jersey, and unfortunately she had left her magazine at the bus stop, which deprived her of some much needed entertainment. She had vowed not to bring any work on the trip, which was a difficult promise for a busy lawyer like her to keep. So instead of magazines or work to occupy her time, she had to enjoy the passing scenery of traffic and old buildings on the ride.

Although she was very close to Amanda, it had been six months since they last saw each other – right around the time Amanda had met her husband-to-be. Still, they kept in contact via email and texting. Sarah blamed her workload for their lack of face-to-face communication.

Her uncle greeted her at the front gate. He gave her a kiss on the forehead, his mustache tickling her skin. He was a jovial man, always welcoming people to his home – even strangers – and greeting them with a warm smile. It was something Sarah always loved about him.

"How are you, my dear Sarah?" he asked, a smile crossing his face.

"I'm doing just fine. What about you, Uncle?" she asked, mirroring his grin. "You still look the same, young and fit."

"Oh!" he laughed, flattered. "I'm getting older, but I'm well, thank you. I'm very happy to see you, my child. It has been ages." He held out his arm and Sarah took it, allowing him to lead her up to the doorway. "Amanda is right inside."

"I'm very excited to see her in her dress." Sarah's smile widened. "I'm sure she looks absolutely gorgeous."

Inside, Sarah made her way upstairs to Amanda's room. She knew her way around the house like the back of her hand, having spent many nights sleeping over as a child and wrecking havoc in the living room trying to make the best fort possible out of blankets, pillows, and couch cushions. Amanda's room was the second door on the right in the upstairs hallway, and the door still had the script writing of her cousin's name carved into it.

Standing at the full-length mirror near the closet was Amanda, and she saw Sarah from the reflection and flashed a smile at her. She wore the classic white bridal dress, beaded at the front with a lace sash and long, trailing veil. As she turned to greet Sarah, the layered dress ruffled softly.

"Wow!" breathed Sarah, shaking her head. "You look so different, Amanda."

Amanda gave her most teasing smile. "So, I had to get married for you to finally find time to visit."

Sarah looked mortified. "I am *so* sorry," she apologized. "You know how much I want to see you. I've been really busy with a new assignment."

"Is that so? I think you're just using your lawyer tricks on me right now."

Sarah laughed. "I'm not lying to you, my wonderful cousin. I am thrilled to be here. And believe it or not," she quickly added, "I left all of my work at home."

"I don't believe that for a second," Amanda replied with another smile. "So, tell me, how do I look as a bride? Good or bad? And no lying."

"Hmm." Sarah put a hand to her chin and circled her cousin, pretending to inspect the lovely dress. Finally, she said, "It's decided. You look extremely hot, sizzling, and sexy."

Amanda laughed and shook her head. "Thanks a lot. I feel better now. By the way, I can't keep it a secret any longer. I'm going to introduce you to someone special today."

"You mean Michael? I'm looking forward to meeting him," Sarah replied. She felt somewhat bad that she hadn't met her cousin's fiancé yet. Six months wasn't exactly a long period of time to date before being married, but Sarah had heard so much about Michael that she knew he would make Amanda happy – whether they were together six months or six years before marriage.

"No, not Michael," said Amanda. She played with her veil as she spoke, tossing the soft fabric and watching it float gently back to her side. "Well, you'll be meeting him, of course, and I know you'll love him, but that wasn't who I was talking about."

"What does he do again?" Sarah quickly asked, interrupting her cousin. It was just like Amanda to try to set her up with someone, and it was just like Sarah to be a little hesitant. Since work occupied so much of her time, she didn't have much room for a romantic life, though she secretly wished it wasn't so ... well, so nonexistent. And while she was grateful of her cousin's efforts to find

her a companion, it was all a little embarrassing.

"Michael? He's a software engineer and runs a business with his friend, for the millionth time." She smiled slyly. "Is that another lawyer trick, trying to change the subject like that? You know, I might be distracted with getting married and all, but I'm not going to leave you without someone to dance with tonight."

"Dance?" Sarah cringed a little. "You know I hate dancing."

"Oh, don't be like that. John is very outgoing. Handsome, too." Amanda winked and turned back to the mirror. She smoothed the skirt of her dress, examining herself one more time. "This dress isn't wrinkled at the back, is it? Ugh, I'm afraid to even sit down in fear of ruining it."

Despite herself, Sarah's curiosity had been stoked a little. She pretended to help Amanda examine the back of the dress for wrinkles, but her mind was elsewhere.

"Sorry, who is John?" she asked.

Amanda didn't reply. She simply flashed a silent, knowing smile at her reflection in the mirror.

＊ ＊ ＊

John stood at the church altar, next to the groom as the best man usually did. Michael was looking good in his tux, an excited smile playing upon his lips. He felt happy for his friend, but also anxious with anticipation. He was waiting for his suspicions to be confirmed, and as the string quartet started the soft pizzicato of Pachelbel's Canon and the bridesmaids emerged from the back, the crowd all turning to watch, he saw *her*. At the front, Sarah started down the aisle holding a bridesmaid bouquet in her hands. She was beautiful in her pale dress,

her hair tucked up over her neck with flowers weaved into the locks. Her lips were shockingly red, as though she had been pulled out of the fifties.

The other girls came out, all lining up across from the groomsmen. The bride emerged to the sound of the Wedding March. She looked lovely, donned in pearly white, and John knew he was supposed to be looking forward, but he couldn't help glancing at Sarah more than once, drawn to her.

Yes, the bride was beautiful, but Sarah was breathtaking.

The priest cleared his throat and finally the ceremony was underway.

"A marriage is a way of accepting love and commitment of a man and woman in front of God, before moving to a new life." He said a few more words, most of which John missed while sneaking glances at Sarah, and continued on. "If there is anyone here who believes Amanda and Michael should not be married today, speak now or forever hold your peace."

The church was silent, a silence so roaring that it made John slightly uneasy. The priest continued. "Let us proceed. Do you, Michael, take Amanda to be your lawful wedded wife? To have and to hold from this day forward, for better or worse, for richer or poorer, in sickness and in health, to love, to honor, until death do you part?"

"Yes, I do," he affirmed with a smile. John could see the excitement in his eyes.

"And do you, Amanda, take Michael to be your lawful wedded husband? To have and to hold from this day forward, for better or worse, for richer or poorer, in sickness and in health, to love, to honor, until death do you part?"

"Yes, I do," Amanda replied.

John let out a sigh. He liked weddings, especially what they symbolized: eternal love, unconditional love. He had grown up with two loving parents who exemplified what it meant to love. He still lived with his adoring, soft-hearted mother, Jessica, whom he was very fond and proud of. He had promised to be there for her ever since his father, Robert, died ten years ago. He had fought a rough battle with stomach cancer and lost. His passing was heartbreaking for the entire family. His parents' love existed "in sickness and in health" until death eventually pulled them apart.

The exchange of rings came and went and the ceremony closed with a passionate kiss between the couple. The crowd erupted into applause and the string quartet burst into music as they made their way back down the aisle, this time as husband and wife.

As everyone made their exit to get to the reception, John tried to walk next to Sarah. Once again, he went unnoticed. He brushed his hand through his hair and craned his neck to find her as she became lost in the crowd.

In the evening, at the reception, John was sauntering by the bar, waiting for another glimpse of Sarah. Almost all of the people at the wedding were at the reception, and some who weren't at the ceremony were present here, probably for the free food and booze. John was about to seize himself a drink when Amanda popped out of nowhere and grabbed his arm. He opened his mouth to speak but Amanda beat him to it.

"I want to introduce you to my beautiful cousin, Sarah," she said.

John's heart skipped a beat. Serendipity. He couldn't believe Amanda was offering to introduce him to the very woman he had his eyes on. "Yes, please," he quietly said, allowing himself to be tugged along by his friend's new wife.

They approached a table where Sarah was merrily chatting away with an elderly man whom John took as a family member. Her eyes alighted when she spoke, her lips curving into a striking smile. His heart elevated.

Amanda cleared her throat, interrupting the conversation. "Sarah, this is who I wanted you to meet, John Deane."

Sarah turned, blushing slightly for some reason. John realized that Amanda must have been trying to set them up, and mentally thanked her. Sarah was looking at him as if she knew him from somewhere but just couldn't place it. Finally extending her hand, she said, "Nice to meet you, John."

He shook her hand briefly, the feeling of her smooth skin sending a rush of exhilaration through him. "Isn't it a coincidence?" he asked.

"Coincidence?" She furrowed her brow.

"I saw you at the bus stop this morning in Manhattan." He shuffled his feet, feeling rather awkward that he had realized this and she hadn't.

Amanda interrupted with surprise. "You've met before?"

"No, no, I just saw her in passing ..." John tried to explain, but he cut his own words short, feeling heat under his collar.

"Oh? Sorry, I didn't notice you," said Sarah, eyeing him with a look of uncertainty. "I didn't realize I was so memorable."

John smiled at her teasing. "You left a magazine behind."

"Oh my god, I was in such a hurry I forgot it." She smiled bashfully and tucked a loose strand of hair behind her ear. "Did you find it?"

"Yeah. I have it if you want it back," he said.

Sarah waved her hand in the air, dismissing the notion. "Oh, don't worry about it. I've almost read the whole thing." She quickly added, "Though, I wish I could have gotten it before the bus ride."

Amanda suddenly decided that this was her cue to leave. "I've got to see some other guests. I'll talk to you later." She squeezed Sarah's arm, gave her a triumphant smile, and dashed away.

"She's trying to set us up, isn't she?" John asked, chuckling a little. He was secretly glad.

Sarah sighed and leaned against her hand. "She does that to me sometimes."

At that moment, the band began to play. People started towards the dance floor, dragging their partners along with them. John – like Amanda – suddenly decided that this was his cue to do something.

"Sarah, would you like to dance with me?" he asked hopefully.

Sarah hesitated, covering her mouth with her hand to hide a shy smile. "No, I can't dance."

"Don't worry. I think anyone can dance with the right partner." He gave her a reassuring smile. "Give me a chance. I'll guide and support you on every step."

She looked surprised for a moment, but her expression was quickly covered by another timid smile. "As long as you promise not to laugh when I embarrass myself," she quietly said.

John gazed dreamily into her bright eyes. He wanted to tell her that she would look lovely doing anything, that she should never be embarrassed. Instead, he slipped his hand softly into hers and led her to the dance floor.

He kept his promise to lead her in every step, and while Sarah stumbled on his toes on occasion, for the most part they were in sync, moving across the hardwood as one. He pulled her closer and said, "See, you've got the hang of it."

Sarah quietly laughed and red touched her cheeks as she let him pull her closer. There was electricity in their fingertips as they touched, a wave of emotion enclosing them as the dance continued on. John's mind was filled with thoughts of her, his emotions leaking into his eyes, and Sarah's shyness had soon withered, becoming just as lost in his gaze as he was in hers.

Two songs had already passed and John and Sarah forgot the music and the people around them. By now, the other guests had circled around them, focused on their passionate dancing. When they finally stopped, Sarah wanting a glass of water, she started at the round of applause they received. She blushed, her shyness returning, and she fled from the dance floor, her hand still locked with John's. She pulled him behind her.

In the safety of the crowd and loud music, Sarah began to laugh. John joined in, feeling completely silly and ... and something else, something he had never felt before. It was a first for him – this feeling – and he held onto it. In his university days, many girls had asked him out, but he never felt interested. He only dreamed of becoming the next Steve Jobs or Bill Gates. Romance and feelings never seemed very important. But when he looked at Sarah, something changed within him, a warmth that he liked.

They spent the rest of the night talking, and John was even able to coax another dance out of Sarah. It was all perfect, and as the hours pushed on, the bride and groom made their flower-laden exit, sending up another round of applause. By this point, John realized he had found someone truly special.

It was not until he glanced at his watch that he realized how late it was. He excused himself and explained that he had a long drive home to Manhattan.

"I have to go, but I had a lovely time talking and dancing with you," he said, faltering slightly on his words. He badly wanted to kiss her cheek.

"Yes, it's been really nice," agreed Sarah, and added, "And fun."

He shook her hand, wishing to feel her warm skin just once more before he left. The breathless feeling returned and he disappeared outside before his urge to kiss her also came back. While walking to his car, he thought of their dance, of how his heart had felt so full and alive in that moment.

And he suddenly realized he hadn't asked for any

of Sarah's contact information. No phone number. No address. Not even an email. He turned to the door, only to see her driving away with her aunt and uncle. He almost considered chasing down the car, but the opportunity was lost.

Sarah Jane Miller. *What a beautiful name*, he thought, as he gazed upwards at the star-filled sky.

And since fate had been so good to him already, he had a feeling he would certainly see Sarah Jane Miller again.

CHAPTER 2

The day was warm, so Sarah left her house wearing a silk blouse and high-rise shorts, her leather handbag tucked delicately into the nook of her arm. Her sunglasses were on, shadowing the world in a brown hue. She felt giddy, happy, and whenever she became this way she felt inclined to get out of the house and go places. Today she decided to visit the mall. A little bit of shopping did wonders to a brain that wouldn't stop thinking about a certain someone.

In fact, she was so busy thinking about her new love interest that she almost bumped into several people on the way to the mall. She tumbled out a few awkward apologies and nearly gasped in surprise when she saw John around the corner. At first she thought she must have been imagining him. There weren't many coincidences in her life. And fate? Well, she was still on the fence with that one.

But there he was, walking towards her in a button-up white shirt tucked into his dark-blue jeans. Even jeans looked professional on him. He had this classy sort of look about him that Sarah loved. Though, he wasn't going anywhere classy today. There was a small, brown dog by his side, its head low to the sidewalk, as if it was sniffing for something.

Sarah's smile broadened when he took sight of her, and his lips curved into a wide grin.

"John, I'm so glad to see you again," she greeted before he could. He seemed suddenly too busy to say "hello" anyway. He was staring intently at her face, and she felt unexpectedly self-conscious about it. Had she put too much makeup on this morning? Had she smudged a bit when she rubbed her eye earlier?

"Sarah, you look gorgeous," said John softly, and Sarah felt heat fill her cheeks. She awkwardly pushed a curl of hair behind her ear and laughed.

"Thank you for the compliment," she replied, and then hurried to change the subject. "Where are you going?"

There was a grim expression upon John's face. "To the doctor's clinic."

"Oh?" said Sarah, curious now, and slightly worried. "Anything serious? What happened?"

John bent down a little and patted his dog on the head. "No, my dog here needs a doctor. I am on my way to the veterinary clinic at the corner."

Sarah glanced down at the dog and saw him sniffing at the sidewalk again. She lowered herself into a crouch and started scratching him behind his ears. "He's very cute," she remarked. "What's his name?"

"His name's Nick," replied John, beaming down at the dog. "He's my best friend."

Sarah smiled. "That's a nice name." She rubbed Nick's back and head for a moment, until the pup started wagging his tail gently back and forth. There was still something wrong, though, as his head kept to the ground. Sarah's brow furrowed. "What happened to him?"

"I don't know." John gave a low sigh. "He hasn't been feeling well lately. His legs seem to have caught some type of infection."

"Oh, that sounds bad," said Sarah quietly, turning her attention back to the poor dog. "He must be going through a lot of pain."

A flicker of fear crossed John's face. "Maybe," he said uneasily. "To tell the truth, I'm kind of scared."

Sarah glanced quickly up, and smiled inwardly at John's openness about his feelings. "Don't worry," she reassured him. "He'll be fine."

Nick suddenly let out a little bark, startling Sarah. John laughed.

"I guess that's the signal to leave," he said. "I'm sorry. I have to get going."

"Oh, sure," said Sarah, a little disappointed that he was leaving so soon. "Please, call me with an update."

An amused look crossed John's face, and Sarah's heart skipped a beat. Amanda had told her he was outgoing, but nothing about his charm.

"Sarah, I don't have your number yet," he said, quietly but hopeful.

Sarah gave an uneasy laugh, forced away her blush, and rose to her feet. "Sorry, I must have forgotten." She reached into her purse and pulled out her phone so they could exchange numbers.

"Thanks, Sarah," said John, once they had swapped. She noticed he kept using her name, as though he liked the sound of it. At least, Sarah *hoped* that was why he said it so much.

"Well, goodbye, John – and Nick." Sarah looked down to the dog, who was staring curiously up at her. She winked at him. "I'll see you again."

She glanced up in time to see John hide a smile.

"Bye, Sarah," he said, starting to walk away. He threw a grin over his shoulder as he called, "Take care!"

Sarah stayed rooted to the spot for a while, watching John until he rounded the corner with Nick, the dog casting inquisitive looks behind now and then. She finally turned, fixing her course to the mall, and was suddenly back to being absorbed with thoughts of John. Giving a sigh, a shake of her head, and a very interesting smile, she pulled open the door to the mall and disappeared inside.

❊ ❊ ❊

The clinic wasn't too busy, so John was sent in right away with Nick. He was ushered into a white room with a single table at the centre, shelves along the walls, counters full of utensils, a few chairs, and a square light that slightly swayed overhead. A doctor met him, shaking his hand briefly before adjusting his rimmed glasses and motioning for Nick to be placed upon the table. He was an older man, which gave John some reassurance because it meant the man had many years of experience in his trade.

As John watched the doctor look over Nick, his earlier fear rose again in his chest. He never liked needles – or doctors, really – and he liked them even less while watching his furry friend being poked and prodded by both. The doctor had cleaned the infected area and put a bandage around Nick's leg. The needle came last and John had to look away.

"What's wrong with Nick, doctor?" he asked. His voice felt hollow.

"Nothing very serious," replied the older man. His voice didn't sound troubled at all, though he had probably seen a dozen cases this week like Nick's. "He has a minor infection. I have cleaned the area and bandaged him up. He'll be okay in a few hours."

John breathed a sigh of relief. "Thank you, doctor." He wanted to shake the other man's hand, but he didn't think that would have been the best idea right now, as the doc was wearing latex gloves that were covered in medicinal cream. "I was really concerned about his health."

"Everyone always is," replied the doctor, flashing a smile and petting Nick's head.

After paying the fee for Nick's treatment, John carried Nick in his arms out of the clinic, giving him behind-the-ear scratches the whole way home.

❋ ❋ ❋

The day passed rather slowly, and John found himself lying on his bed, tossing an old baseball again and again into the air. Nick was feeling better, just as the doctor had said, and the dog was now pacing back and forth across the bedroom, sniffing at whatever sparked his curiosity. John sighed and returned the baseball to the end table by the bed. It was covered in awards, medals, and trophies. Not all sports, though. Some were sports, collected throughout high school and university, but most were related to software engineering. He had ranked high in his class at university, scoring most awards. He still kept his computer books, too. They were stacked on one of the shelves by his desk, some of them collecting dust. His laptop was open, though the screen had faded to black some hours ago, and disks lay unorganized in the basket

attached to the desk. Pictures were hung over the desk, some university days – him in his graduating gown, him and Michael by the school entrance, him flashing his diploma – and others of his childhood.

Reaching into his pocket, John pulled out his phone. He flipped over onto his stomach and scrolled through his contacts to find Sarah's name. He pressed the call button and waited for a response. At first, no one answered. He felt a little discouraged and wondered if she didn't want to talk to him, but he shook that thought from his head, knowing that *she* was the one who had asked for updates. So he dialed the number again.

❋ ❋ ❋

A beep woke Sarah up from her sleep. She blinked sleepily and rubbed her eyes, pulling herself into a sitting position on the bed. The noise was gone and she looked tiredly around, wondering where it had come from.

Her walls were covered in paintings, some she had made herself. She liked how a paintbrush felt as it graced a canvas, how the color splashed against the white. She didn't paint as much as she used to, though. Her job was very demanding and interfered with her hobbies.

On the nightstand, next to a framed photo of her – one that had been taken by the Hudson River in New York at sunset – the clock read 10:45. Sarah groaned and was about to go back to sleep when she heard the noise again. It was her cell phone, buzzing noisily on the desk. She pushed back the bed covers and stumbled across the room to her phone.

Her heart skipped a beat as she saw John's name flash across the screen. Replacing her grimace with a smile, she clicked the "answer call" button.

"Hello!" she greeted, and then wondered if she had sounded a little too happy.

"Hello, Sarah. This is John," said the voice on the other side of the phone.

"How is Nick doing?" asked Sarah curiously.

There was a moment's pause. "He's feeling better. Listen." Sarah did, and she could hear soft growling in the background, meaning Nick was playing with something. She laughed. "What about you?"

"I'm fine, and you?"

"I'm okay," said John, and just as Sarah was wondering if any of this was going anywhere, he continued, "If you aren't busy, do you want to meet tomorrow?"

Sarah found herself sitting on the edge of the bed, hanging her feet off the side and swinging them distractedly back and forth. "You mean ... like a date?"

She couldn't help the smile that crossed her lips.

"Yes, it's a date," said John.

Sarah found herself giddily laughing. "Okay."

"Then, are you free tomorrow?" asked John hopefully.

Sarah bit her lip and tried to stop her girlish laughter. "I'll manage the time."

"Great." She heard a trace of excitement within John's voice. "So, are we going to meet again?"

"Yeah, sure," confirmed Sarah.

"Okay, sounds good."

❉ ❉ ❉

The first thing John decided to do for his date was get a haircut. His hair was getting out of hand lately. He could easily brush his hands through it and style it back like he had walked out of a medieval movie. So heading straight to a salon was currently in his best interest. He was handed over to a young, energetic man, barely in his twenties, but had a dozen certificates over his section of the salon. John felt he was in good hands. He also knew the hairdresser was chatting away about something or another, but John found himself unable to keep up a conversation. His fingers were busy at his phone, texting away to Sarah.

* * *

The water was scorching hot, the steam rising above the shower walls and flooding the bathroom. Sarah had her face amidst the pouring liquid, allowing water to caress her cheeks, forehead, and lips. It felt heavenly. She rarely had time to enjoy her showers, so every time she got a chance to linger, she did. Soon the shower was over, though, and she pushed back the curtain and wrapped herself up in towels. Her hair threatened to escape beneath the cloth, but she secured it with a firm twist and headed out towards the bedroom.

Her phone was flashing on the bed and she picked it up, flipping it open to see a new text message. It was John, of course, messaging the time and place of their date. Giving an excited grin, Sarah dried off and got dressed in front of the mirror, carefully choosing what to wear. John had chosen a classy restaurant for their date,

so she needed something elegant. Sarah found that her style of clothes was very modern, so finding something classy wasn't *too* hard. She pulled a long, black dress out of her wardrobe and held it up in front of her in the mirror.

A smile graced her lips.

*** * ***

When John saw Sarah enter the restaurant, he felt like he did that day at the bus stop. She was beautiful, radiant. She had chosen a slinky, black dress that hugged her figure nicely, with inch-wide straps and a v-shaped back. Her auburn hair was curled to one side, a few strands escaping on the other, caressing her cheek. Her makeup was soft, giving her eyes a gentle feel. John felt the breath leave his lungs.

She sat down, smoothing out her dress and began talking about the trip to the restaurant. John was vaguely aware of a waiter lingering by them, asking him something. A menu was placed before him and he managed to snap back to reality.

"And for you, ma'am," said the white-suited waiter, holding out a menu to Sarah.

"Thank you," she replied, tilting her head a little forward. She took the menu and spread it open before her.

"Would you like to start with some drinks?" asked the waiter, glancing a little irritably at John, though he hid it well with a charming smile.

"No, thanks," said John quickly, though he turned to Sarah just as fast, realizing that he had forgotten her opinion. "What do you think?"

"I'd like some soft drinks," she said.

The waiter bowed and left them. They checked over their menus for a while, chatting back and forth about the food and what they might order. When the waiter returned, John ordered a steak with a vegetable side and Sarah decided the same. They threw in a bottle of wine and some cheesecake desert, also.

"I'm excited!" said Sarah suddenly, her eyes shining. "This is our first date!"

John felt his mouth turn dry and he tried to find his courage. He was always an outgoing person, always able to talk a room full of people into absolutely anything, but there was just something about Sarah that made him nervous. "I want to make this day memorable, Sarah," he managed to say.

Sarah's cheeks were turning red and she was smiling. The sight of her so vulnerable gave him the courage to reach into his jacket and pull out a small velvet-covered box. He pushed it across the table towards her and watched as she opened it, her eyes filling with surprise.

"This ... this is beautiful," she breathed, lifting the necklace out of its container. It sparkled in the low light of the restaurant. John rose from his chair and moved to Sarah's back. The hair tickling the back of her neck caused him to feel tenderness towards her, and his heart raced as his fingers graced her skin as he fastened the necklace around her neck. He returned to his seat. "Thank you for this wonderful gift, John," she continued, and squeezed his hand. "I'm speechless."

"It was my pleasure."

He convinced her to allow him to take a picture of her on his phone so he could keep it as her contact picture, and they began to eat when the waiter returned with their food. Once everything but the desert was eaten, Sarah

leaned forward on her folded hands and stared tenderly into his eyes.

"I never imagined we would become so close in just a few days," she said softly.

"It feels almost magical," said John quietly, studying Sarah's bright, playful eyes. "We only met a few days ago, but ... but it feels like we've been together for years." He paused, wondering if he should comment more on it, and decided to keep talking anyway. "It doesn't feel like a coincidence." Another pause, and then, "Do you believe in soul mates, Sarah?"

He looked up and across the table at her, judging her reaction to his statement and wondering if she now thought him crazy. Though, a serious expression had crossed her face and he knew she had thought about this before tonight.

"I don't know what's happening to me since I met you at Amanda's wedding," she admitted slowly. "I don't know if it's love. Why do I want to be intimate with you? Why do I want to be committed to you? Why do I want to be attached to you?" She shook her head. "It feels like I have no control over what happens. I don't know if this is infatuation or love!"

John smiled softly, feeling his heart contort at her every word. "I feel the same, Sarah. I might be the wrong person to ask for advice in this matter, so I don't know what to say to you." He thought on it for a moment, and replied in his soft voice. "Actually, love is something that is beyond us. We can't anticipate love. When, where, and with whom we fall in love is coincidental and wonderful for the same reason."

Sarah was staring at him with mixed amazement and surprise. "Perhaps you are right," she whispered, and a tender smile began playing on her lips. John copied her smile as they clinked their glasses together. They spent the rest of the evening at the restaurant taking turns devouring the cheesecake and chatting away.

CHAPTER 3

With the success of their last date and the promise of another, John and Sarah found themselves walking hand-in-hand at Central Park the following day, despite the weather warning of high winds. The sun was shining and the sky was void of clouds, though the air was fierce and Sarah clutched her scarf as they moved towards the lakeside. The wind died down a little once they drew closer towards the trees that were scattered about the park, and they stood within the shade, protected from the wind and still able to clearly see the lake.

The shimmer of light from the sun caused the water to quiver in beautiful waves. There were people on the other side of the lake, tall shadows to those on this side, and they moved stealthily up and down the shore. John watched them for a few moments, lost in thought, until Sarah let go of his hand. He peered down to see that she was rubbing her eye, wincing a little.

"Are you okay?" he asked.

"There's something in my eye," she replied.

"Here." John moved her hand away and inspected her emerald eyes. There was something in there—a piece of dust or dirt or something equally irritating—and John unbuttoned the sleeve of his shirt and used the end to wipe it out. "All better?"

Sarah smiled, her face flooding with color. *How embarrassing*, she seemed to be thinking. John saw nothing of the sort. He saw the love of his life, his soul mate, and she was everything he had ever wanted in a woman.

"I love you so much," he breathed, stroking her face with the back of his hand.

Sarah looked up from the ground, her smile widening. "I love you, too."

John pulled her in towards him, feeling her body heat mix with his own, and placed a long, lingering kiss upon her forehead. She shivered a little and he draped his arm around her shoulder, guiding her down closer to the lakeside.

They lay side-by-side on the lush grass, staring up into the clear sky and holding hands. The San Remo apartments were in the distance, towering high into the air like skyscrapers from their relaxing position. John studied Sarah in the afternoon sun, allowing his eyes to wander over her yellow, silk dress and auburn hair. The sunlight seemed to soak into her very flesh, making her appear younger, freer. He liked that look on her, the look of someone who could do anything, who could be anyone, who could go anywhere.

She seemed to notice he was staring and she winked and smiled.

"My dear, don't you seem romantic today," she mused.

John grinned and rubbed his fingers along her hand. "Maybe."

Sarah leaned towards him. "Are you going to tell me why?"

John pretended to look hurt. "When a beautiful woman accompanies a man to the park and is seated so close to him, can he not feel romantic?"

Sarah smirked and returned back to where she was lying, giving a sigh. "All right." After a few moments, she gave him a sidelong glance. "Are you really not going to tell me?"

John laughed quietly. "Ask all you want, clever girl. I'm not telling. You'll just have to wait and see."

The wind had died down quite a bit now and the sun was out in full force, burning across the lake and Central Park like a tidal wave. Sarah removed the shawl of her dress and threw it aside before leaning onto John, draping her arm across his chest. He felt his heartbeat increase rapidly as she stroked her delicate fingers across his face, tracing his features. And then she leaned forward and kissed him. Not a fierce or fast or forgettable kiss, but a slow and passionate one, soft and warm like the sun.

Unable to control himself, John rolled her over and lay on top, kissing her by the lakeside. She was warm and beautiful and *his*. He could feel her breathing, her heart against his chest, her fingers as they wound in his hair.

After some time, he drew away, remembering that they were in public and were probably creating a scene. No one wanted to see a couple making out in Central Park—even if it wasn't an uncommon sight. John owed his pride a little more than that.

"Come with me," he offered, standing up and stretching out his hand.

Sarah took the offer and allowed him to help her up. She brushed the strands of grass off her dress and John checked his own clothes before guiding her down towards the lake. They stopped just a few inches from the water, their shoes crunching against the pebbles underneath. John bent down and picked a few flat ones up, judging their size as he chose. He passed half to Sarah.

After Sarah's several failed attempts to skip the rocks off the clear surface of the lake, John laughed and told her to watch.

"The trick is in the motion of your wrist," he explained, and then showed her, adjusting her hand and how to hold the stone.

Even after the demonstration, she still couldn't get it, and they ended up laughing over her clumsy efforts, John teasing her as they made their way out of the park. The winds were picking up again and they decided to move their date indoors.

The Metropolitan Museum seemed like a good place to go, so they went to the Met museum and they were whisked away to the art gallery. John took Sarah's arm through his own as they entered the building. It was busy, like always, and tourists flooded the area, mixed in amongst the regulars. John heard cameras clicking and tour guides announcing their next destination. They decided not to go on a tour but drift through the crowd and observe on their own. Many paintings—oil, pastel, acrylic—were hung in the gallery, bearing pictures John couldn't even begin to decipher. There was also a large collection of sculptures—figures of men and women and even animals, all crafted with sincere likeness to realism. Other pieces of art were scattered here and there: fountains, hanging objects, relics, and recreations of history. It was beautiful place, and one that John thoroughly enjoyed.

Finally, John found Sarah stopping beside an exquisite oil painting of a woman bending over a desk with a paintbrush in hand. It was labeled "Young Woman Drawing, 1801".

Sarah smiled briefly up at John before turning back to the image on the wall. "This is a painting by a French woman, Marie-Denise Villers. It's believed to be a self-portrait of the artist. The painting was attributed to Jacques-Louis David at one time, but was later realized to be Villers' work."

John had to admit, he was impressed. He wondered if he should have known that or if it just wasn't common knowledge, that Sarah was just an expert in art. "Interesting. Have you been here before?"

"I visit a few times a month," replied Sarah.

"You have a lot of interest in art, I see," said John. "Why not an artist or an art historian instead of a lawyer?"

Sarah gave a slow shrug. "I'm not sure." She smiled up at him. "Art's just a hobby, I guess. Everyone has to be passionate about something."

I see it in your smile, thought John to himself, and he caressed her cheek with his thumb as he returned her warm grin.

"You look prettier when you smile," he whispered.

Sarah beamed and looked away, flushed. "Thank you," she said.

They left the oil painting behind and found new portraits to discuss and dissect. It seemed in that moment that there was nothing more relaxing than walking with Sarah in the museum, sharing opinions and feeling her fingers intertwined with his.

❋ ❋ ❋

The sight of her always took his breath away, though she didn't know it. William remembered her at the bus stop, all dressed up with plans swimming in her head. Now she was simply wearing an old T-shirt and trousers, sitting outside on her porch with a paper in one hand and a cup of steaming liquid in the other. He figured it must have been tea. She was a tea sort of girl.

His footsteps on the wooden steps alerted her and she looked up, smiling when she recognized him. William joined her at the small table, nestled in the corner by her pots of flowers and hanging birdhouse. It was empty for as long as he could remember, though she kept it there anyway, being the hopeful sort of person she was.

"Sarah … how is everything?" he asked, taking off his coat and sitting.

"Everything is fine," she replied, sipping her tea and placing the cup upon the table.

"I was trying to reach you all last night," he began, "but it was constantly busy."

"Yeah." Sarah mindlessly shifted her cup with her index finger. "I was talking to someone."

William's heat skipped a soft, painful beat. "Someone special?"

Sarah's face suddenly seemed to light up. She tried to hide the shy smile that crossed her lips but William caught it. He had known her so long that he would notice the slightest change.

"Well, were you going to hide him forever?" William forced out a laugh. "What's his name?"

"John Deane," answered Sarah, finally allowing her smile to blossom. "We're dating."

"When did you first meet him?"

"At Amanda's wedding. He's Michael's closest friend." Sarah's face took on a thoughtful look. "But, he said the first time he saw me was at the bus stop that very morning."

William held back his grimace. He remembered that morning, too, but he didn't recall another man at the bus stop. He recalled seeing Sarah, remembered being captivated by her words as if he had wandered into a dream that was over far too fast. He wanted to tell her that, but he felt it would be pointless.

"Really?" he said instead, compelling himself to smile. "I would like to meet him someday." Not because he wanted to get to know the man who was dating the woman he loved, but because if he couldn't have her, he needed to know that someone good was with her.

"Sure, why not?" Sarah's smile grew wider. "I'll tell him about you. Maybe you can find yourself a date and we'll all hang out—"

A cell phone rang. William knew it wasn't his. Not his ringtone. It was Sarah's, and he just caught the name 'John' flashing upon the screen before she stood up and wandered across the porch, talking in whispers.

William watched her, watched the way she smiled at whatever John said, the way she laughed and curled her pretty hair around her fingers. She turned back towards him, but he hid his frown and nodded politely towards her.

With someone like John in her life, she could never know how he felt, and he wouldn't be so selfish as to tell her.

* * *

Often William wished that the relationship between him and Sarah was something more than just friendship, especially at times like this. She had made him lunch and was now standing at the sink in her apron, washing up dishes from breakfast. There was a song on her lips and she was humming merrily away, entertaining herself while he ate.

Suddenly the song broke and she spun around, leaning her elbows back against the counter.

"Bill, can I ask you something?" she said, rather

impulsively.

William looked up from the table, questioningly. "Yes, of course."

"Have you ever fallen in love with someone?" The words slid out of her mouth like rushing water, unable to control itself.

William blinked, startled by her question. "Well …" He put his fork down slowly, measuring her expression. "Maybe."

This answer was a little surprising to Sarah, and he knew why. He usually told her everything.

"Who is she?" Sarah demanded.

William watched as she hurriedly dried her hands on the dishtowel and tossed it onto the counter. "It's complicated," he finally said.

"Complicated how?" wondered Sarah aloud, drifting towards the table. "Is she in love with someone else? Is she married? Is she too young?" Sarah laughed and placed her hands against the back of a chair. "Or you just don't want to tell me her name?"

William smiled and leaned across the small table towards her. "It's you, Sarah."

He wasn't really prepared for her reaction, which was a mix of surprise and amazement. Her hands had gone white on the back of the chair.

"You ... you're kidding, right?" she whispered, frowning.

No, I'm not kidding, William felt like shouting, but he knew he was losing her.

"Don't be so serious, Sarah!" he exclaimed, laughing. "I'm only joking."

Sarah's hand flew to her chest. "Gosh, Bill! You scared me!" She scowled and batted his arm with her open palm. "I was shocked, you know. I thought you were serious." She sighed and pulled out a chair to sit down for lunch. "You'll find someone special in your life someday, Bill, and she'll love you. It doesn't matter how long it takes you to get there."

Sometimes he wished her words were the absolute truth, but he feared he would never love anyone like he loved Sarah.

"Life is unpredictable," he told her. "It doesn't always go according to plan. And you never know what's coming."

Sarah folded her hands together. "According to my gathered wisdom, life is full of beautiful moments." She quietly laughed. "Just live your life to the fullest and do what you love." She squeezed his hand. "That's all that matters, Bill."

William looked slowly down at her hand and gave a small smile. "You're probably right. Let's see what happens." Feeling another wave of emotion rising up, he stood and began to get Sarah some of the food she had cooked.

"That's okay, I can do it myself," said Sarah.

"Think again," said William, motioning for her to sit back down. "You've already exhausted yourself with all the kitchen work. Let *me* serve *you* for a change."

Sarah shook her head and laughed, falling back into her chair. "Okay, I give my consent."

❋ ❋ ❋

The past few days had gone by much too slowly, and John was anxious to speak with Sarah face-to-face again, though it was late and he couldn't run out to see her. He was sitting in his bed, his pillows bundled up behind him so he could be relaxed and still prop his computer upon his lap at a reasonable angle. He was waiting for the home screen to load, allowing everything to start up before he logged onto his messenger program to send a message to Sarah.

Only a few more minutes now ...

❋ ❋ ❋

A beeping noise echoed in the living room and

Sarah hurried over to the couch, seeing a message window pop up on her computer screen. She flung herself onto the leather seat and picked up the laptop, eager to chat with her boyfriend.

Boyfriend. That word still made her giddy. She had never had time for boys in the past, and now it seemed she had all the time in the world.

"Starting ... video ... chat," Sarah spoke aloud as she typed in the message. She clicked the 'video' button in the corner of the message box and waited for John to pick up the call on the other end. He did, and she saw his face upon the screen, as handsome as she remembered. His hair was a little wet from a recent shower and his shirt was hanging loose, giving him a delicate, attractive sort of look. She felt herself smile before knowing it.

"I was dying to see you today," she stammered out. "I'm glad we can at least chat online, even when we can't see each other throughout the day."

"Me, too," said John, elated. "I find it extremely difficult to stay away from you, Sarah. I feel like you're around me all the time."

Sarah's heart leapt within her chest. She smiled warmly. "I feel the same way, sweetheart."

John's face on the other side was a little blurry —the result of a somewhat slow internet speed—but Sarah could make out every detail: the line of his jaw, his curved cheeks, his dark eyes, the twist of his lips when he smiled. He was smiling now, softer than usual.

"Sometimes I feel like it's our destiny that we met, instantly liked one another, and fell in love," he said quietly, gently.

The past few months rushed through Sarah's head like an angry tidal wave, reliving each and every moment that she and John had shared. They were all happy memories, mixed with love and affection.

"It's still like a dream to me," she admitted. "I never thought to be in a relationship someday."

"To be frank, it was my dream to have someone like you in my life," confessed John, his smile softening even further. "And now I feel like my dream has come true."

"Really? Have you dreamt to date anyone before?"

John seemed a little embarrassed. "If you truly love someone, you shouldn't doubt them. I was busy most of the time with computers and programming. I never really had time for girls."

"Sorry, honey," said Sarah with a laugh. "I trust and love you. You needn't take it seriously."

"Oh, oops." John also laughed. "I guess it's true: it's difficult for men to understand women."

"That's because they're dumb!" said Sarah. "Women are clear and to the point. They let people read them. They don't play 'hide and seek' like men."

"All right, all right," said John, laughing. "Let's just leave that topic where it is before we start fighting! I don't want to start a 'men vs. women' debate. It may strain our relationship."

Sarah grinned and leaned further into the couch. "I love you, honey."

"I love you, too, my sweetheart!" he rubbed his eyes and said. "I'm feeling pretty tired now, though. Should we put this off until tomorrow?"

"I seem to have developed insomnia," confessed Sarah.

"Insomnia?" John sat straighter. "You never told me."

Sarah smiled. "The moment I close my eyes, I see you and sleep vanishes. I'm awake the entire night, revisiting our memories together. The night seems to stretch on forever."

John sighed. "That isn't good for your health. I'm going to be with you forever, love. Just close your eyes and sleep. I'll be here tomorrow and the next day and the next."

"I know," said Sarah softly. "Good night, honey. Take care."

"Sweet dreams," said John.

"You too, dear."

Sarah switched off her laptop and moved it aside.

She sat on the couch for a long while, dreading going to sleep. Finally, she stood up and got ready for bed, slipping into PJ's and sliding under the covers. Though, try as she might, she could not fall asleep. Her mind was too busy, too focused on John.

And—miles away—John was in the same predicament, too busy thinking of Sarah to rest his weary mind.

CHAPTER 4

John was sprawled out on his bed, his face buried into his pillow, and his short pajama pants curling uncomfortably around his knees, though he didn't seem to notice. Jessica Deane had pushed open her son's bedroom door after knocking a few times, wondering if he had slipped out before she had woken up or if something was wrong. But he was soundly asleep, his breathing a gentle hum.

"John? Wake up, John! It's late!" she urged him, quietly so he would not be startled by her voice. He didn't respond. He didn't even flinch. He seemed to be completely taken by whatever dream filled his sleep. She wondered if he was stressed about work or something else, and worry flooded through her, as it did all mothers.

Giving a quiet sigh, Jessica left the room, closing the door softly behind her.

A car alarm was going crazy outside, and John groaned, stuffing the pillow over his ears and face, hoping that the sound died away soon. It did, but by then John realized that something was amiss. The sun was pouring a little too freely into his room from the half-opened window, the curtains steadily drifting back and forth. John rubbed his eyes and glanced down at the watch Sarah had given him.

Giving another groan, he jumped out of bed, tossing the blankets aside in the process, and strolled out into the hall and into the bathroom. He closed the door lightly behind him and wandered over to the sink, where an oval-shaped mirror hung just above it. John lazily reached for his toothbrush, still stuck in sleep-mode, and forced some toothpaste out of its tube onto the brush.

As he scrubbed his teeth clean, he could not help but glare at himself in the mirror. As much as he enjoyed talking with Sarah, he should not have stayed up as late as he had – or forgotten to set his alarm clock. Or maybe he had set it and was so tired that he absentmindedly turned it off when it sounded earlier this morning. Either way, it was still his fault and he would be late for work because of it.

After polishing up his teeth, he ran the water warm and splashed some up onto his face, washing away his sleep. He wondered for a brief moment while drying his face if his mother had tried to wake him up, and felt a little guilty. He placed the towel back on its rack and inhaled deeply before leaving the bathroom, a little flutter of anxiety travelling down his spine at the thought of his conversation with Sarah last night. They had talked about love, deep and intense love, and he felt that way towards her. He knew he would always feel that way.

Back in his bedroom, John searched his wardrobe for his work clothes. In all honestly, most of the clothes he owned could be considered "work clothes", but there were certain shirts he liked to wear to his day job: dark, classy, button-downed shirts with nice collars. He picked one of those out and quickly changed, casting another look at his wrist to check the time. He really didn't see

the point it in anymore. He knew he was late, but he looked anyway, perhaps out of habit.

His mother was waiting for him in the kitchen, hovering over the stove with her hand on the grip of her favorite frying pan. John seated himself at the table before she turned around, and he heard her humming softly under her breath. There was some sort of strength to his mother, some sort of intensity that he loved about her. When her husband had been battling sickness, she had been the glue to hold them together, to keep them strong.

The death of his father had strained her somewhat since. She was in her mid-sixties, her dark hair all intact and few wrinkles spreading across her face, but sometimes she looked much older, as though the demons of her past were rising up in her memory. He helped her however he could. Sometimes he woke earlier to cook for her, but he was scolded afterwards. He then thought that perhaps being busy was the best medicine she could ever have, that looking after her son, the remainder of her family, could be all the help she needed to overcome her grief.

"How are your projects going?" asked Jessica, moving from the stove to the table. She flipped a few fried eggs and several pieces of bacon onto his plate, and then mimicked the action to her own dish. The food looked delicious, as usual. The eggs were just a little crispy and the bacon was burned perfectly.

"Very well," replied John, picking up his fork. His mouth watered at the smells before him. "But it's a challenge managing so many projects at the same time." He gave a quiet sigh as he stuffed a piece of bacon into his mouth. "Sometimes it's boring ... and frustrating."

"Any update?" she continued with her questioning. She reached around him and poured hot coffee into his mug. He instantly picked it up, desiring the bitter taste of it on his tongue, even if it was still steaming. Coffee was always welcome after sleeping in so late, especially when he knew he was in for a scolding when he arrived at work, or at least a headache, or two.

"We have a new client," said John, draining some

more of the coffee. It tasted heavenly. "It's going to be a big project for us. I'm very happy with our progress."

"That sounds good," said his mother, relief flooding into her voice. She cleared her throat, as though trying to hide the fact she had been momentarily worried. "I'm happy that you're happy. It's important to do what you like doing."

John placed his mug down by his plate, a small smile lingering upon his lips. "It was always my dream to work on such innovative projects and lead in the technology world." His smile slightly faded. "But I still have dreams that have not taken shape." He thought of Sarah, then, as he said it, and he wondered what their future together would hold. "I don't know when I'll be able to fulfill all my dreams." He gave a quick laugh, trying to bring a smile back to his mother's face. "God knows when all of that will happen."

His mother gave his hand a gentle squeeze. "You never know until you give something your best and keep working at it. Follow your dreams no matter what, John."

John turned his smile soft, and squeezed her hand back. "It means a lot, Mom. Thanks."

After he finished off his breakfast and another cup of coffee, he kissed his mother on the cheek and headed towards the doorway, snatching up his briefcase by the stairway as he went.

"I need to go now. It's getting late," he called over

his shoulder.

Jessica was already moving plates to the sink, dipping them into water. He could hear them clinking. "Okay, take care!"

He watched her for a moment before he vanished outside, remembering her strength and resolve in the worst of times, when his father was dying and the world seemed to be splitting in half, and left with a smile on his face, knowing that everything would be all right.

* * *

Work was about as busy as usual, the office buzzing with chatter and ringing telephones. John's laptop was on, a spreadsheet filled with numbers flooding the screen, and although he was staring at it, he wasn't really paying much attention to the chart. His cell phone was up to his ear, and he was waiting for someone to pick up the call. He knew he shouldn't be making personal calls while on the job, especially after coming in late, but he wanted so badly to hear her voice that he wouldn't be able to work anyway with her on his mind.

"Hello, Sarah!" he greeted, as she answered in her cheerful tone. He loved her voice, always sweet and sincere. It was one of the many things he enjoyed about her.

"How is everything going?" she asked, and he suddenly had a mental picture of her twisting a phone cord around her fingers, distractedly like in an old movie, although he knew she was on her cell phone.

"Fine," he answered. "And you?"

"I'm ok," she said. "What plans for the day?"

"Well, are you free?" John could barely contain the excitement inside of him. He idly crossed his fingers, hoping that she would be available to see him.

"Yeah. I'm planning to go to a movie," she said, a bit of smile in her voice. It warmed his soul. "I bought two tickets for us."

John's heart leapt forward in his chest. "Which movie is running at the theatre? And what time will the movie start?"

Sarah laughed on the other line and he wondered if she was laughing at his eagerness, which caused him to flush a little. "At 6:15 PM. It's a romantic movie."

There was the sound of heavy footsteps behind him, but John hardly noticed. Someone was probably just passing his desk. "Sounds great, Sarah. I'll talk to you later."

He ended the call and looked up in time to catch sight of Daniel Smith lingering near his table. He leaned against the side and grinned over at John, his rimmed glasses perched high on his nose. He was older than John, somewhere in his early thirties, but Daniel was every bit twenty at heart.

"You have a second?" he asked, still with that stupid grin plastered upon his face.

John motioned to the chair across from him. "Please, have a seat."

"Thanks, dude." Daniel twisted the chair around and leaned his arms against the back as he sat down. "So, can I ask who Sarah is?" John couldn't help the bashful smile that fluttered to his face at the mention of her name, and Daniel instantly noticed it. His grin widened, which only caused John to become more awkward. "When are you going to introduce me to her?"

"Maybe someday," replied John, a little irritated at himself, but mostly at Daniel. "Let's get to the point."

Daniel seemed a little disappointed, but his face turned into his serious business side. "Did you call our client, Mr. Graham?"

The call had completely slipped John's mind, as did many other things when Sarah was dancing around in his thoughts. "Not yet. I'll call him soon. Please, send me all the related files you have."

Daniel rose from the chair. "Okay, I'll send them over right away." He paused before he left. "When is Michael coming back to the office?"

John shook his head, a little clueless about the

subject. "No idea. He's still on his honeymoon." He rubbed the bridge between his eyes. "Things are getting more complicated in his absence."

"Yes, you're right," agreed Daniel, shifting his shoulders back.

John watched his co-worker and friend drift off towards his own desk, a light rhythm to his steps, and wondered exactly how crazy it would get with Michael gone. He missed his best friend, and work always seemed to get done fasted with him around. Now John's hands felt sluggish, his heart jolted randomly, and his mind was too preoccupied with his new love life to get anything done.

He really wished Michael would come back.

When John met Sarah at the theatre, he had been overwhelmed with his desire to see her again. And she had rushed up to meet him, flinging her arms around his neck as though they hadn't been together in weeks. She had thrown on a dark jacket with a high collar, a shirt with a flowing front, and sleek, black pants fitted with a thick belt. John was convinced that she looked good in just about anything, and had complimented her on the outfit, getting a compliment back in return, though he knew his clothes rarely showed the same diversity as hers.

They sat in the dark theatre with a few snacks, mostly candy as Sarah liked theatre treats, and cuddled closely together. Halfway through the movie, when the actor on screen finally realized that she was in love with her best friend, Sarah clutched onto his hand and leaned her head against his shoulder, not moving until the credits were over.

John peered down at her before the lights were turned back on and she gazed back at him, sharing his warm smile. He so badly wanted to kiss her, but they were getting in the way now, others back in the row wanting to get out. They rose and left with the crowd, hand in hand.

❋ ❋ ❋

The movie had been wonderful and John had been wonderful and this entire night is just wonderful, Sarah could not help but ramble in her mind. She was walking down the nearly empty street with John, her arm through his. The streetlights shone their way forward, along with the seldom passing car. He had offered to walk her home and she had agreed, desiring his company more than wanting to catch a cab alone.

He was a large part of her life now, something special that she didn't want to lose. She loved being near him, being with him. He made her smile, made her laugh. She hardly had this much fun before meeting him, always too busy with her job to take any time out of her day to entertain herself. Now she had John and she loved him more than anything.

"Thanks, Sarah," said John suddenly, nearly startling her. "I liked the movie. It had a nice ending."

"It did," agreed Sarah, snuggling closer to him. She could see her house now, looming up before them like a terrible nightmare. She didn't want this night to end, not yet. But now they were standing at the front gate, the metal slightly rusted along the bottom. Sarah took a quick look at the door and then to John. "Won't you come inside?"

John stared intensely at her for a moment, causing her heart to beat frantically against her ribcage. There was something strange in his eyes, some form of frustration or passion. "Not tonight," he finally said, though he seemed like he didn't want to say it, which pleased Sarah. "I'll come another time. It's already late. Mom will be concerned." He gave her a strained look. "I have to go now."

Sarah knew that he lived with his mother, taking care of her after the death of her husband and his father, but would she really be that concerned if he stayed out too late? It seemed a little odd, but she didn't question it. Maybe there was something going on that she didn't know, something that would cause his mother to stress.

"Okay," she said slowly, disappointedly. "Bye."

"Take care," said John, and he seemed about ready to leave, to walk away and desert her at the gate, but he took a step forward and drew both his hands around her face.

She felt the heat of his fingers before anything else, and then his lips as he gently kissed her. She moved her hands up through his dark hair and he pulled her closer against him, embracing her for a long moment. She listened as their hearts seemed to beat as one, pounding rapidly.

Then the kiss was over and John was walking back down the street. Sarah drew her arms around herself, shivering a little even in her jacket. The touch of his warmth had vanished. She watched him for a long time, until he was a speck at the end of the road and then faded into nothing.

CHAPTER 5

The room was mostly dark, save for the light of the moon shining in through the open window. Then the room filled with man-made light, illuminating the hand-painted furniture, canvases upon the walls, and the woman lying in her bed. Sarah flicked off the lamp again, reminding herself of a game she played when she was a child, though she did it then for curiosity. Now she was just bored—and unable to sleep. Her mind was swamped with thoughts of John. Dear, sweet John, who had taken her on a perfect date earlier tonight.

Heaving a sigh, Sarah finally gave up and turned off the lamp. She lay back in bed and stared up at the dark ceiling. Sleeping was hard when your mind was preoccupied with other thoughts. She just wished it would keep quiet and leave her alone when she was trying to get some rest.

❖ ❖ ❖

John's eyes casually drifted back to the television as he slid his shirt on. There was some sort of sitcom on. He didn't recognize it, but it seemed pretty funny from the glimpses he caught of it. He buttoned up his shirt as he watched the characters onscreen, rushing from one location to the other.

"When are you leaving?" his mother called from the other room.

"At ten-thirty," answered John, pitching his voice above the television. It wasn't very loud—he didn't like loud TV—but his mother's hearing wasn't as great as it once was. "Are you making breakfast?"

"I'm cooking now," said Jessica. "Tell me what you'd like."

"Something quick." John straightened his tie and pulled on his jacket. "I'm in a hurry today."

"Okay."

John wandered over to the mirror and brushed back his hair with his fingers. He fixed his collar and gave a smile to his reflection. He looked good, very businesslike, which is exactly how he wanted to look today.

After eating a fast breakfast and giving his mother a quick kiss goodbye, John ventured out to his car and threw his briefcase inside. The ride to work was mostly quiet, the only music playing towards the end of the drive as the radio station turned from talking to singing shortly before eleven. John left his car in the parking lot of his office building and took the elevator up, checking his watch several times and tapping his boot impatiently against the floor.

He made his way to the conference room, where everyone was already gathered. It was small group, all seated around a circular table. Some were John's clients, while others were partners. John placed his briefcase at the empty spot at the table and immediately got started on his presentation.

He was showcasing a new type of software, one that he and Michael had been working on before his wedding. It was now completed and ready for marketing and distribution. John didn't waste any time with his presentation, but when everything was said and done it was nearly six o'clock. He loosened his tie and packed up his things before leaving the building, heading back to his car in the parking lot.

It was then that he noticed the jewelry store across the street. John paused, the wheels turning in his head. He abandoned his car for the moment and headed for the crosswalk.

❀ ❀ ❀

I really don't like the mall's autumn clothes lineup, Sarah was texting Amanda as she flipped through the weekly flyers. She had a subscription to all the stores, though she hardly got the chance to go out shopping with work tying her down as it did. Yet she still enjoying looking and talking about it to pretty much anyone. Today Amanda was her victim, though her cousin was saved when the doorbell rang.

Sarah leapt up from the couch and peered out the window to see John standing on the porch. She smiled giddily and flung open the door, happy to see him unannounced.

He laughed. "I'm sorry I came without a call. I was busy all day in a meeting. I just wanted to see you. I couldn't help myself."

Sarah was still smiling. "No, it's okay." She extended her hand to the room beyond. "Please, come in." She shut the door behind him as he wandered inside. "To be honest, I was expecting you to drop by, and I'm happy you've finally decided to come inside."

John shot her a sheepish look before dropping down onto the couch where Sarah had just been sitting. She removed the magazine from the sofa and lay down with her head on his lap, staring up into his face. He looked handsome today, very proper and professional, and his hand running through her hair felt very nice.

"I think love is the purest and most beautiful of all feelings in this world," he whispered. "What do you think?"

Sarah thought upon it. "I think ... love is love, and it isn't comparable to anything."

John smiled softly down at her. "Hmm, maybe. By the way, I have something for you."

A curious gleam filled Sarah's eyes. "What is it?" she asked.

From within his jacket, John pulled out a small box. He opened it to reveal a sparkling necklace. Sarah sat up and brushed back her hair so he could link it around her neck. It felt cool against her skin, and she touched the necklace and studied how it looked around her neck.

"You look stunning," complimented John.

Sarah beamed and jumped to her feet, happy that he thought so. "I also have a surprise." She winked and disappeared into the kitchen before returning with a bottle of red wine and two glasses. She passed one to John before popping open the wine and filling his glass. "Now, enjoy your drink!" She poured herself a glass and tapped it against his. "Cheers!"

"Cheers!" echoed John, laughing. He swirled his wine within his glass and took a sip. "Mmm, it tastes really great."

"The best," agreed Sarah, and she sat with her legs crossed upon the couch, eyeing John through the corner of her eye as she sipped her drink.

After a few glasses, Sarah was feeling a little light-headed and giddy. John didn't seem to be doing much better. He laughed more, and she even caught him telling jokes a few times. Eventually, they found themselves

kissing upon the couch, unable to withstand each other any longer, though Sarah had tried hard not to jump him while he was here. They made their way to the bedroom, linked within each other's arms, and John slid his jacket off, letting it fall to the floor.

The bed was soft and inviting, and Sarah found herself smothered with heat in John's embrace. His kisses were slow and passionate, making her heart race and her body ache. He pulled off her shirt and kissed her neck, his hands gentle along her sides.

And then both had their clothes on the floor and entered into a new level of their relationship. Sarah felt him everywhere at once; his presence was overwhelming. Her fingers dug into the sheets when they merged as one, and she felt his hands grip hers, calming her heart. He whispered her name and kissed her slowly, and the night progressed like a dream.

❋ ❋ ❋

Groggily, Sarah opened her eyes and grimaced as the sun struck her square in the face. She rolled over to see John in her bed, still asleep and breathing softly. The light caressed his face in gentle ways, enveloping his skin in a warm glow. Sarah watched him for a little while, memorized by the way he looked, before taking a long breath and sliding out of bed. She fetched a clean T-shirt out of her dresser and threw on some underwear, a little modified, before venturing downstairs.

Everything was so silent, and Sarah noticed that it was still early in the morning. She pulled open the fridge door and took out a fresh bottle of wine. She glanced into the living room to see that they had drained the other one.

The dining table seemed a good spot to sit, so she climbed up onto it and poured herself a glass of wine, though not actually drinking it just yet. Her knees pulled up to her chest and she stared at the floor, reflecting upon the previous night. She had made love to John. She had taken a huge leap in their relationship. They hadn't gone on many dates and she certainly didn't know everything there was to know about him. Yet it didn't feel wrong or too soon for some reason. It was a puzzling feeling.

❋ ❋ ❋

The water felt good as he splashed it upon his face. John dried off his skin with the hand towel hanging nearby and looked into the mirror. His stomach was in knots—nervous, yet excited, knots. They had taken a big step last night, though he wasn't sure how Sarah felt about it. Was she happy or upset or …?

"John? Are you awake?" she called.

"Give me a minute!" John called back, his heart doing a somersault at the sound of her voice. "I'll be out soon!"

He finally left the bathroom, deciding he couldn't hide in there forever, and wandered down to the kitchen where Sarah had just finished cooking some eggs and toast. She placed two plates on the table and gave a small smile.

"Last night," began John, a little bashfully, "I was …"

"It's okay," interrupted Sarah, still smiling.

That smile seemed to relieve him. "Thanks," he breathed, falling into the chair before him. "I'll be out after I eat."

It was all he could do not to stuff the food down his throat. Some part of him felt a little regretful. He had wanted their first time together to be a little more romantic, a little more planned out than it was.

"I'll call you tonight," promised Sarah, once he was at the door and they were both done eating their breakfast.

"Okay," agreed John. He kissed her cheek and left.

***

On the way back to his apartment, John stopped for a moment to stare across the street. He usually wasn't overly interested in cars, although his love for design sometimes got the better of him. This particular Mercedes Benz parked directly across from his house was the latest model, some name he had forgotten, but its design intrigued him. He stared at it a little more, thinking about how fantastic it might look parked in front of his apartment, and silently headed inside. He tossed his coat on the couch and hoped that his mother was still asleep. Unfortunately, she noticed the sound of the door opening, even after John had tried to conceal it so well.

"John, where were you last night?" demanded Jessica. "It's not like you to not come home."

"I was at a friend's house," replied John, pulling off his tie. It was starting to choke him.

"A girlfriend?" inquired his mother, her voice sharp.

John sighed in irritation. "Oh Mom, don't be ridiculous. Why does it matter where I was?"

"I am just asking," said Jessica, a little defensively. "I noticed something strange about your behavior lately."

John didn't reply to that.

"I am only thinking about you and your career,"

said his mother quietly.

Though, John didn't feel like continuing the conversation. He simply headed upstairs to his bedroom. He didn't want to tell his mother about Sarah. Not yet, anyway. She had always believed in his work and understood the lengths he went through to secure his position in his field, though now that he was with Sarah, he couldn't bring himself to tell his mother that she felt more important to him than work. He wasn't sure if she would be disappointed in him or happy that he had found someone so special. So he wouldn't tell her yet. He had to wait until the perfect moment to reveal his news, maybe when she understood a little better that he could handle two commitments at once.

And he could. He definitely could.

❋ ❋ ❋

Night had fallen, and everything was cool and quiet again. Sarah walked leisurely into her room, her cell phone in her hands. She had not called John all day, as she had promised to call at night, and now she was a little nervous about it. He filled her thoughts constantly, and she had put off going to sleep because she knew she wouldn't be able to fall into dreamland very easily. She knew it wasn't healthy, but she couldn't help it!

Looking down at her cell, Sarah finally decided to call. His number was on speed dial, so she pressed the button and held the phone up to her ear. As she listened to the sharp rings go through, Sarah moved towards her window and pulled back the curtains to glance outside.

The sky was clear, no clouds blocking the stars or moon. It was a glowing half-moon, lingering high in the atmosphere, surrounded by a crowd of twinkling orbs. Sarah stared upwards for a long moment, only the sound of someone answering her call bringing her back down to Earth.

After waiting for Sarah's call and not receiving it, John decided to just go to bed. She had probably fallen asleep or forgotten to phone him. These things happen. He was a little afraid that after what had happened the previous night she didn't want to call him, that she was angry or upset or not sure about what was going on between them.

Yet just as he was drifting off to sleep, worry clouding his thoughts, his cell phone buzzed loudly upon his night table and he reached over to claim it. It was Sarah—the shot of her at the restaurant was her call picture. He hurriedly clicked the answer button.

"Hello, Sarah," he greeted. "I thought you'd be asleep by now. It's eleven-thirty."

"I was trying to sleep," admitted Sarah, "but I can't. I think about you at every moment—and I have to go to court tomorrow for an important case!"

"You should get some sleep before it gets too late," instructed John, slightly relieved that she wasn't upset, though now feeling a different set of emotions for her wellbeing. He sighed and rubbed his eyes. "I worry about you sometimes, Sarah. You can't stay up all night thinking about me. You need to control your emotions."

"You're everything to me," whispered Sarah into the phone. "I don't care about anything else."

"Don't be crazy," said John, angry now. "You have a whole life to live. What if I die someday, leaving you? What will happen then?"

"Don't ever say that again!" snapped Sarah, her voice hollow. "I don't want to live my life without you!"

John sighed again, but brought a weary smile to his lips. "Sarah, unexpected things happen in life sometimes. You just have to accept them." He checked the time on his phone, a little anxious that she was up at this hour with somewhere important to go to tomorrow. "Anyway, it's really late. You should try to sleep. Maybe after talking you feel a little tired?"

There was a slight pause. "Well, I do feel a *little* sleepy," agreed Sarah quietly.

"Okay." John laughed. "Take care, and sweet dreams."

John hung up the call and placed his cell phone back on his night table. He relaxed back into bed and shifted his arm under his head. A smile came to his face as he closed his eyes. He felt entirely happy at this moment. Sarah was contented with their relationship, which doused all the worry from his mind. He felt a little silly for being so anxious all day, but he soon forgot about it, drifting off into pleasant dreams.

CHAPTER 6

It had been a tiring day for Sarah. All morning she had been contained within court, working with a client and pushing as hard as she could to sway the case in her favor. She won out in the end, through a series of lucky turns, and now court was dismissed for the day. She was glad it was all over. Her suit was much too warm. Several times she had felt overheated while talking, and sitting still had been torture. Now she was outside in the cold breeze. Winter was here. It seemed to have crept by overnight.

At the bottom of the courthouse stairs, Sarah spotted William. He raised his eyebrows in surprise when he saw her and climbed halfway up the stairs to meet her.

"Hi, Sarah," he said, and joined her as she descended. "How's your day going?"

"Nothing too special, just another case," replied Sarah. "Pretty average so far."

"I see. Do you need a ride home?" he questioned.

"No thanks," said Sarah, smiling at his gesture.

"John is coming to pick me up."

"Oh." William mimicked her smile. "Well, okay then. Bye."

Sarah waved. "Bye."

William wandered off down the street while Sarah finished her trek down the stairs to the sidewalk. She lingered there for a while, glancing from her phone to the street every now and again. She checked her email, sent a few texts, played some random flash game sent by a friend, and then looked at the time. John was running incredibly late.

Sarah sat down on the bench near the base of the stairs and crossed her legs before returning to her phone. She refreshed her email and leaned back on the seat, a little bored. Finally, she saw John's car coming up the road and she slowly stood up from the bench, her feet and legs tender from standing most of the day.

"I am extremely sorry for being so late," said John, once he had gotten out of the car and approached her. He gave her a quick hug and kiss.

"It's okay," said Sarah, allowing John to open the car door for her. She got inside and waited for John to take the driver's seat before continuing the conversation.

"You look tired," he commented, after studying her face.

"It's been a long morning," said Sarah with a sigh, "and I'm starving."

John smiled as he pulled back out onto the street. "Well, do you want to stop somewhere and eat?"

"No." Sarah shook her head. "I can't think about going anywhere right now. Let's just go to my place and make something."

"Okay," agreed John.

❊ ❊ ❊

Since they had started dating a few months ago, John had been secretly practicing cooking so that he could surprise Sarah at some point. Today seemed like the perfect day for it, though even with his fancy cooking apron and Sarah's kitchen utensils, he still needed a cookbook in front of him. He had thrown some chopped onions and garlic into the sauce he was now stirring, and he hoped—he *prayed*—that it was good.

"Here, want to try some?" he offered, lifting up the spoon towards Sarah. He was a little nervous as she licked the sauce into her mouth and swallowed, shifting her eyes back and forth as if debating whether it was decent or not.

"It's delicious," she finally said, and nudged John in the ribs with her elbow. "I see you're a good chef."

John gave a nervous laugh. "No, not yet. I'm still learning, but I'm glad you liked the sauce."

"Everyone has to start somewhere," said Sarah, and smiled as she took another taste of the sauce.

They finished up in the kitchen, arranging the plates and food upon the table, and then began to eat. Sarah had changed out of her suit and was now in a regular T-shirt and jeans. She sighed with delight when she took her first bite, and John wasn't sure if she was teasing him or if he had actually done a good job with the meal. Either way, she looked happy and that was fine enough for him.

❊ ❊ ❊

The next few months seemed to fly past in a blur to John. Things at the office were going smoothly, his relationship with Sarah had never been better, and he was even thinking about putting down a lease on that Mercedes Benz he had an eye for a while back. He decided he would call Sarah later and ask what she thought about it, as he felt their relationship was serious enough for her opinion on things like that now. Buying a car, after all, was a big deal.

Looking down at his watch, John saw that it was almost six o'clock. He was leaving work a little early, but honestly he had nothing else left to do for today that would get done in the next ten minutes, so he pushed open the office main doors and stepped outside.

To his surprise, Sarah's car had pulled up at the front of the building and she was getting out. She was also dressed nicer than usual, wearing her best coat and a little more makeup than she typically applied. Though, she still looked about as beautiful as she always did.

"Hey, you're here," he said, a little amazed. "Are we going somewhere?"

Sarah grinned deviously. "Maybe. Maybe not. I'm not telling you anything."

John laughed. "All right, sounds good. Let's go to maybe nowhere."

Sarah smiled again and returned to the driver's seat. John shuffled into the car, as well, tossing his case in the back. Sarah's car was nice and tidy, her CDs stacked in a row in the middle of the seats, all her paperwork bundled up in the backseat, and her line of sunglasses clipped to the sun visor.

John kept his eyes on the street as she drove, reading the street names and trying to figure out where they were going. It took a while to get to the place where Sarah was taking him, though, so he had plenty of observing to do. It was a small but cozy restaurant with an outdoor seating arrangement in the downtown area, flowers next to every table in attractive pots. Sarah parked the car across from the restaurant and they both got out.

Inside the restaurant, John detected some sweet and spicy aromas, along with the sound of gentle, romantic

music. It was a classy place, with hanging pots of brightly colored flowers, deep, lush paint tones, and high-quality service.

"Sarah Miller," said Sarah to the finely dressed waiter at the door. He nodded and extended his hand, motioning that they should follow him.

They were taken to a table in the back, hidden from view by most other sections of the restaurant. It was already set, with a bottle of white wine at the center, beautiful flowers, lighted candles, and a tag with Sarah's name upon it. The waiter removed the paper once they sat down and promised to return in a moment with their food.

John couldn't for the life of him remember what today was. Had his birthday come and gone so soon? Or was it *her* birthday? He surely hoped not. He didn't have a gift bought. Before he could panic too much, however, Sarah began to speak.

"Happy Valentine's Day, Honey," she said, taking his hand. "I love you."

"Damn it," swore John, shaking his head. He felt like an utter fool now. "I completely forgot. I'm sorry. Happy Valentine's Day, Sweetheart. I love you, too."

Sarah gave a beautiful smile. "I'm a last minute planner. I'm sorry I couldn't manage anything more."

"Your surprise is perfect, as is your planning," said John, giving her hand an apologetic squeeze. "I'm the one who should be sorry. I forgot what day it was."

Sarah waved her hand in the air, brushing the matter aside. "No, it's all right. I understand that you've been really busy with work lately."

John sighed in relief. "Thanks, Sarah."

"Just 'thanks'?" She pouted.

"So, what are you expecting?"

As John looked into her eyes in the silence that seemed to swallow up the music, he swore he could see each and every thought she possessed. There were a million of them at once, and they were all for him.

"I want you to promise that you'll never leave me alone," she whispered, gripping his hands firmly.

"Okay," said John, a little uneasily. He leaned forward and locked his gaze with hers. "I promise I will never leave you alone. I will be your shadow and walk with you, and I'll love you forever."

Sarah flushed at his words, even after all this time. "Thank you, John. I love you so much, and I want to spend my life with you."

"Me, too," agreed John, a little light-headed at what she said. He gave a quiet laugh. "My happiness feels rather limitless today."

Sarah giggled. "I feel the same way."

John studied her curved face, so delicate and perfect, her bright eyes and ruby lips, and the flow of her auburn hair as it travelled down her back. It had grown quite a bit since he had first met her, and she often kept it up, just not tonight. Under her coat was a flowing, dark shirt with several necklaces travelling down her front, and it brought out her pale face even more.

"You look so beautiful, Sarah," he whispered.

"Thank you," she quietly replied, smiling at the compliment. "You look extremely handsome yourself in that suit."

John laughed and leaned back in his chair as the waiter returned. It seemed Sarah had ordered the food in advance, as well. He was a little surprised to see his favorite foods appear, but when he saw the mischievous

glint in Sarah's eyes, he knew it really wasn't last minute planning at all. She had been keeping track of what he liked to eat—and apparently his favorite kind of romantic music, judging by the songs playing in the background. She was altogether too perfect for him, and he loved her for it.

Outside, the thunder clashed violently overhead and lightning zigzagged through the dark sky, sending waves of light into the dim living room. Jessica moved back to the kitchen after retrieving a glass she had left by the couch and slid it into the sink with the other dishes, hearing it tumble to the bottom. The kitchen window was also open, the curtains flapping in rage from the severe wind pouring in. Jessica sighed and moved over towards the window. There was a bit of water along the sill underneath, built up from the rain sneaking in, so she wiped it away with a cloth before shutting the window.

Instead of going straight back to the sink to finish up the last of the dishes, Jessica noticed a strange car pulling up to the apartment. She leaned a little closer towards the window to see John sitting in the passenger seat. Beside him, driving the car, was a young lady with reddish-brown hair. Jessica had never seen her before, but she had a feeling about who she was. Her son had been displaying some odd behavior lately, behavior she recognized well, though she had been waiting for him to tell her about it. Maybe tonight he would.

❋ ❋ ❋

"It's still raining," commented Sarah, as she looked out the window of the car. The rain had come on rather

suddenly while they were driving back to John's apartment, and now thunder and lightning had joined it.

"You have to walk me to my door," said John teasingly. "It's the rules of dating, remember?"

Sarah scowled and pushed open her door, and then screamed as the rain poured down over her. John laughed and jumped out of the car, too. He grabbed Sarah's hand and pulled her along towards the apartment entrance. A flash of lightning startled them both as they dashed under the protective roof of the entryway. Sarah was breathing heavily, as was John, and they laughed together. Both their clothes were soaked through, and Sarah's hair was now stuck around her face. John pushed some strands back, grinning in amusement at her.

Then he leaned forward and kissed her deeply upon the lips, tasting both her and the raindrops that had stuck upon her skin. He felt her arms slink around his neck and her fingers stretched through his damp hair.

After a moment, Sarah pulled away. "I have to go," she said, a little disappointedly. "Work, remember?"

John didn't want to let her go just yet, though. He pulled her closer towards him, feeling her body as it pressed against him, and moved in for another kiss. Yet the rain had stopped and Sarah seemed to notice.

She looked up before their lips met and smiled at the retreating storm clouds. The first stars had begun to appear through their dark covering.

"Looks like I'm free to go," she said quietly. "I have to go, John. It's late."

John reluctantly let her go, watching as her hand slipped out of his. "All right," he finally said, defeated. "I'll see you tomorrow."

Sarah smiled and nodded before heading back to her car. John stayed where he was for a few moments. He watched her start up the engine and drive off before heading inside and up the stairway.

Before he got to the top, however, he paused in alarm, seeing his mother standing in the open doorway. A wave of shock and shame passed through him for a few seconds, eating him up inside, and then it disappeared, dissolving into pure regret. He should have told her before now. This wasn't the way his mother was supposed to find out about Sarah.

Lingering on the stairwell wasn't going to do either of them any good—or progress the situation —so John ventured up towards his apartment and passed his mother, not meeting her gaze. He slumped down onto the couch as she closed the door.

"Who was that girl?" asked Jessica quietly, as she pulled the lock across. It clicked into place, securing the apartment.

"Her name is Sarah," replied John, feeling even guiltier now. He figured it was better late than never to tell her, and since she had already seen Sarah kissing him, there was no point in denying her existence any longer. It wasn't like he was trying to hide her forever, though.

"Why didn't you tell me about her?" continued Jessica, her voice lowering. "Does she know about me?"

"I'm sorry, Mom," said John, rising from the couch. "It's not what you think, honestly. I-I just didn't know what to tell you, especially after you've been so good about my career. But I was going to tell you soon, I promise."

Jessica seemed to feel a little better after hearing that. She gave a small smile and looked towards the kitchen, where bubbles appeared to be slowly popping in the sink. "Do you love her?"

"Yes, Mom," answered John, a little coyly.

"Well, bring her home sometime," instructed Jessica, taking on a motherly tone once more. "I want to meet her."

John smiled, relieved. "Of course, Mom. Anytime you want."

After their conversation was over, Jessica returned to the sink where she had most likely been before the awkward scene, and John ventured upstairs towards his bedroom. He got undressed and climbed into bed, weary from everything that had transpired today. Though, he wasn't too tired to stay up for a while still, thinking upon the evening's events.

I want to spend my life with you, was what Sarah had said, and John couldn't agree more with that statement, for he wanted the exact same thing.

CHAPTER 7

It had been a few days since John's mother had found out about Sarah. He had been tossing ideas back and forth in his head since then, wondering how he should introduce his girlfriend to his mother. Those ideas ranged from fancy dinners to an evening to the art gallery to a stay-at-home gathering. Honestly, he shouldn't have been so nervous about it. Sarah was a wonderful person, and his mother would love her.

Yet it had been rather silent between them since then—John had told Sarah that his mother had caught them, which she became quite embarrassed about and apologized over and over. Now they were out walking in the park, enjoying a cool but sunny winter's day, encompassed in that same silence. John thought it was about time he fixed it.

"My mother wants to meet you," he blurted out, breaking the tranquil walk.

Sarah jumped a little at the sound of his voice. "Your mom?"

"She knows you're my girlfriend," said John, remembering the conversation he had with his mom that night. "I told her about our relationship."

"Oh." Sarah nodded sensibly. "That's good—I mean, it *sounds* good." She fidgeted awkwardly with the strap of her purse. "This will be the first time I meet her. I-I'm a little nervous."

John quietly laughed. "Don't be so nervous. My mom is really friendly." He nudged her with his elbow. "She'll be *very* happy to meet you."

Sarah gave him a weak smile. "You're probably right. I guess I'm just scared that she won't like me."

"That's ridiculous," said John, frowning at Sarah's lack of confidence. He took her arm and looped it through his. "My mother is a soft-hearted, caring woman. She'll love you."

Sarah sighed and chewed at her lip. "Then why do I still feel nervous?"

John stopped walking and turned Sarah around to face him. Her cheeks were red from the cold air and he placed his gloved hands around them, locking their gazes. "Sarah," he started, his voice soft, "don't worry about it. You're the most beautiful, intelligent, charming girl in the world. She can't reject you. *Trust me.*"

Sarah's cheeks grew redder still and she directed her gaze elsewhere. "Thanks," she whispered, and her smile grew confident once more. "When should I come by?"

"Any time at all," replied John, moving his hands away. He linked their arms together again.

"Can I meet her right now?" asked Sarah.

John was a little surprised by this, but he mimicked Sarah's smile and nodded. "Sure. Why not?" His mother was probably at home, anyhow. She didn't leave the apartment much, other than to go shopping or visit the neighbors. She was quite contented with her television shows and reading.

"Okay." Sarah's eyes grew determined—the same way they looked before she tackled a troubling case. "Let's go."

I suppose this would be a challenge to Sarah, thought John considerately. *I met a lot of her family at Amanda's wedding, but she has yet to meet mine.*

They left the park behind, heading back towards the exit and to where John had parked his car. His apartment wasn't overly far from the park, but it was winter and he didn't feel like hiking through any snow to get anywhere when he didn't have to. So they climbed inside the vehicle and Sarah cranked up the heat and rubbed her hands in front of the fans to warm her fingers. John had on the leather gloves Sarah had bought him a few weeks ago, and he was pleasantly surprised by the amount of warmth they contained, even on the coldest days. She was always so thoughtful, his Sarah, and he knew his mother would love her. Sarah's worrying was absolutely pointless.

❊ ❊ ❊

Oh dear, thought Sarah, once John's car had pulled up to his apartment. His words back in the park had brought her comfort, but now she was starting to feel anxiety building in her stomach again. Horrible thoughts raced through her mind, bullying her into thinking that his mother wouldn't like her, or she would demand that John would stop seeing her, or she would refuse to even look at her because of what she had witnessed the other night.

Sarah gulped as they approached the front door. They should have told his mother about their relationship a long time ago. The awkward event on the doorstep would have never happened then, and perhaps she wouldn't have felt so anxious about her first meeting with his mom. It was too late for regrets, though, so the only thing left to do was to face the situation head on. *Just like a trial*, Sarah reminded herself, but she couldn't

remember the last time she had felt so nervous about a case.

John knocked three times on the door instead of going inside, and Sarah glanced up in distress at him. He ignored her anguished gaze and simply smiled, displaying his confidence. The door opened and a dark-haired woman appeared. She looked surprisingly young despite her actual age, with few wrinkles and no grey hairs. Sarah immediately stuck out her hand in greeting. John chuckled.

"Sarah, let me introduce you to my mother, Jessica Deane," he said. "And Mom, this is Sarah."

"Hello!" blurted out Sarah, flushing a little. *Oh dear, you're embarrassing yourself, Sarah.*

Jessica was not flustered at all. She took both of Sarah's hands within her own and then hugged the other woman, smiling all the while. "You are such a lovely girl, Sarah!" she exclaimed, which caused Sarah to blush even more. The older woman spread out her hand towards the apartment. "And John—what a surprise! Please, come inside. I'm very happy to finally meet you."

"I-I've been looking forward to meeting you, too," stammered Sarah, moving past Jessica and into the kitchen. She had never been inside John's apartment before, so her sense of direction was rather aimless. It looked nice and cozy, though, a touch no doubt acquired by Jessica.

"Excuse me, ladies," said John, walking past them both. He paused at the stairwell. "I have to change out of these clothes, so I'll leave you both to talk alone for a little while."

"Okay," said Sarah, a cold shiver running down her back. *You're leaving me alone with your mom?* Well, she couldn't be frightened now. She at least had to pretend to be brave. "That's fine."

John smiled warmly at her before vanishing upstairs, jumping two steps at a time. Sarah swallowed anxiously and turned to Jessica, who was hovering near the kitchen counter with a smile similar to her son's upon her face. It seemed to bring peace to Sarah's mind.

"Would you like anything to drink, Sarah?" she asked. "Tea? Coffee?"

"Oh, no thanks," replied Sarah, holding up her hand. "I'm okay for now."

"All right, just let me know if you want anything." Jessica sat at the table and Sarah quickly joined her. "So, Sarah, what do you do?"

Sarah guessed John hadn't told his mom much about her, which meant he intended for her to talk about herself. She would have to scold him about it later, and almost laughed aloud at his little scheme. "I'm a lawyer," she answered.

"And your parents?"

My parents ... Sarah lowered her gaze to the table. She hadn't thought about them in a while. John preoccupied most of her time and when she was with him she didn't think upon the past so much. "I lost them in a car accident five years ago," she quietly replied.

Jessica looked a little aggrieved and her eyebrows

crunched in distress. "I am extremely sorry. Please, forgive me. I didn't know that." The older woman wrung her hands together and then placed them flat against the table. "I can understand what you must have gone through—what you're still going through. I lost my

husband to tragedy, too."

Sarah looked up from the table. "What happened?" she chose to ask. John had mentioned his father had died a while back from illness, but Sarah didn't know all the details.

"Well, he had cancer." Jessica's eyes softened and Sarah figured she was recalling a very painful memory. "He survived twice with chemotherapy but the third time he succumbed to it."

"Oh, I'm sorry," said Sarah quietly. She cleared her throat a little and decided it was high time to get off the sad topic of death. "I've been all right since my parents passed, and I see John has good support behind him, as well."

This brought a smile to Jessica's face and the conversation began to go down a different—less depressing—path. The two talked for quite some time, discussing each of their lives. John was taking his time upstairs, though Sarah figured he was on his laptop and completely ignoring them until he decided they had gotten to know each other well enough. She smirked at him as he finally reappeared in the kitchen, letting him know that she had caught on to his crafty scheme.

"I'm ready to go," she said, checking her watch. It was getting late and she had promised herself she would pay her friend William a visit later. She turned to Jessica before rising from the table. "Thank you for the chat. It was lovely."

"You're welcome," replied Jessica, grinning. "You can come by whenever you want."

Sarah returned the smile. "I will, and thanks for being so nice."

"Do you need a ride?" asked John, reaching for his coat on the wall.

"No, thanks," said Sarah. "I can find my way back."

"I think he should drive you back," said Jessica, glancing towards the window. "It's getting dark out, after all."

Sarah also looked outside and then decided against walking. "All right," she agreed, and then turned to John. She hadn't told him she was planning to visit William later, so she figured she would just have to bring him along. "Let's go."

"Be safe, you two," called Jessica as they left the apartment.

It had been a long day at work, and William was happy to finally be able to sit back and relax. His guitar had been stuffed away in its case for far too long now, so he decided to take it out and retire in the drawing room for the rest of the night. There were a few songs he had been meaning to practice in his spare time, so he thought he would work on those first for a few hours and then shift over to something new. He had no work in the morning so he planned on staying up late to enjoy his hobby.

"Needs a little tuning first," he mumbled, as he strummed his thumb across the strings. The pitch sounded a little out of synch. He reached into his guitar case and pulled out his tuner, then positioned it on the coffee table in front of him. He felt a little guilty, allowing his strings to go so far out of tune.

Yet he didn't get time to fix the sound when the doorbell rang. William frowned in confusion, wondering who had swung by this late, and laid his guitar on the couch.

"Sarah?" William stared out onto the porch in amazement. When he had opened the door, he didn't expect to see *her*. "What a surprise! I didn't know you were dropping by!"

Sarah laughed and pulled John out of the shadows and into the light of the doorway. "Well, I'm not alone. John decided to come along with me."

William hid his grimace and pulled it into a smile. "John … well, it's nice to finally meet you."

John stuck out his hand and William took it. "You, too. How are you?"

"Fine." William moved aside and held the door open for them. "Please, come in."

He watched as they entered, Sarah's hand locked with John's, and knew that this was going to be a long visit. He shut the door behind them and moved to the drawing room to put his guitar away. Then he ventured into the kitchen to prepare some food and drinks. Sarah joined him after a few minutes, offering to give a hand with the whiskey.

"Bill is my buddy," she said to John, once he had also made an appearance in the kitchen.

"Yes, we're best friends," added William, as he passed Sarah the glasses. He mentally added that anyone who swung by his home and knew exactly where everything was in his kitchen deserved to be called a "best friend". "It's been three years since we first met."

He realized then that he didn't know much about John, other than that Sarah loved the man—something he didn't like in the least. "What do you do, John?"

"I'm a software engineer," replied the other man, taking a sip of his whiskey.

"Wow, that's great," said William, grudgingly impressed. He figured he needed a way to keep in contact with this man, seeing how Sarah thought so highly of him. "I might need your help in the future to develop a kind of ... client management software. Here, this is my business card." He reached into his back pocket and pulled out a card, always having a few on hand, and passed it to John. "Can I get yours, as well?"

"Oh, sure." John pulled out his wallet and retrieved a card to pass to William. He then inspected the other's card, nodding slightly. "So, you're also a lawyer. I'll have to give you a call if I need help sorting out any legal issues."

William winked towards Sarah and lifted his glass to his lips. "Sarah is a fantastic lawyer. As long as you have her, why would you need me?"

Sarah hit his arm with the back of her hand and scowled. "Oh, stop it. And quit discussing work, you two. Just enjoy the drinks!"

William laughed and turned back to his glass, an ache growing in his chest. He hated seeing her with John, but there was nothing he could do. Sarah was in love with the man, and she had never shown interest in him. Though, he had never really given her any signs to indicate how he felt. Maybe it was his own fault. Maybe if he had expressed his feelings earlier ...

He suddenly lifted his glass to John, pulling forth

another fake smile. "John, you're very lucky to have someone like Sarah in your life."

"Oh, stop ..." Sarah blushed and smiled down into her glass, and William felt pleased that his compliment had warmed her heart, even if it wasn't the same sort of warmth that John gave her.

"I completely agree with you," said John, and he wrapped his arm around Sarah's shoulders. He looked back to William, and the latter could have sworn that he saw some sort of gloating in the other's eyes, though maybe he imagined it. "What about you, William? Are you seeing anyone?"

William swallowed back a harsh mouthful of whiskey. "I haven't been lucky enough yet," he answered, swerving around the truth. "I'd rather focus on my work for now."

Sarah laughed and nudged William in the side with her elbow. "What a liar! He's much too smart for a question like that. He wouldn't *really* share such a personal thing with us, because that's what he's like."

Oh, Sarah, thought William. *If only you knew the truth.*

And he downed the last of his whiskey.

CHAPTER 8

Jessica was busy sweeping the kitchen, humming to the soft melody playing over the radio. The dishes were done and the laundry, too, but she had saved the sweeping for last, wanting to enjoy her midday music without the noise from the dryer or the sink to interrupt. She peered outside to see that it was a beautiful day and she thought she might go visit some friends when she was finished, but at that moment the phone near the fridge rang and she abandoned her sweeping momentarily to go answer it, setting the broom against the counter.

"Hello, Deane residence," she said into the receiver. There was no caller ID on the phone, as it was an old model, and as much as John wanted her to upgrade it, she liked the feeling of being surprised when a familiar voice answered on the other line.

"Aunty?" It was Michael, her son's best friend. He was close to her now, too, of course, as she had invited him over many times to eat with the small family. She enjoyed company, and Michael was a sweet boy. "How are you doing?"

"I'm fine," she replied, smiling though she knew he couldn't see. "What about you, dear?"

"I'm fine, too," said Michael, but he sounded like he wanted to get through the formalities very quickly. "Aunty, where is John right now? I've been waiting for him for the past two hours, and I tried calling but his phone is out of service range. Is he at home?"

Jessica stopped twisting the phone cord around her fingers and stared at the wall, anxious now. "John said he was going straight to work when he left."

"Well, he isn't here," said Michael, a little annoyance leaking into his voice. "We *had* an important meeting earlier, and he knew that." He sighed, filling the receiver with the sound of his heavy breath. "I don't know what's going on with him. This is the second time it's happened, though he managed to catch the last meeting at the last moment. Now he's just not here. He isn't giving much concentration to work lately, and—honestly—I'm a little worried about him."

Jessica swallowed and nodded. "Yes, it isn't like John at all to miss work like that. I'll try to get in touch with him."

Michael sighed again, this time with relief. "Thank you, Aunty. I'll talk to you later."

"Okay," said Jessica, her voice quiet now. "Take care, Michael."

She then hung up the phone and retreated away from the kitchen, forgetting about her last chore. She sat on the couch in the living room, a nervous knot within her stomach. It wasn't like John to miss work. Maybe once—a long time ago—he would have acted that way, but he was different now, better. She chewed at her thumb and nervously shook her head.

No, her boy couldn't go down that path again. She wouldn't let him.

❋ ❋ ❋

It was Thursday, and the only good shows on television on Thursdays were already over. Sarah had been out of the house and had missed them, so now she was absentmindedly flipping through the channels, trying to find a good program to watch. There were so many cooking and reality shows these days, but she wasn't

much interested in any of them. She had about as much

'reality' as she could get in the courtroom, listening to the

lives of others every day. She didn't need to watch a TV show where people were struggling with far less important things, such as boyfriends, clothes, or money. No, she liked suspense and crime related things, so she left the channel on some criminal investigation show, allowing her eyes to drift between that and the book on her lap.

It was not long before she heard the doorbell ring, and she bookmarked her page and placed her book to the side, rising from the couch to answer the door. She knew it wasn't John, as he was busy in a meeting and would most likely be working into the afternoon on whatever new idea the company was now developing, and she knew Bill was absorbed in a case right now, so her usual guests were off the list.

To Sarah's surprise, it was Jessica, John's mother, who was standing on the doormat, wearing a light coat and a beautifully colored hat. Sarah smiled brightly. She hadn't seen Jessica in quite some now— a week, she supposed—and she was glad that she was here now.

"My god, what a surprise!" Sarah moved aside and let Jessica enter her home. She took her hat and coat and hung them up and then proceeded to hug the older woman. "Come in and sit down."

"Thank you, Sarah," said Jessica, and she drifted into the living room. Sarah could not help but note that the woman seemed a little off today, perhaps a little distant and even … sad?

"How are you?" she asked, after they had both taken a seat upon the couch.

"I'm fine. You?"

Sarah gave a single nod. "Good."

There was a moment of silence afterwards, where neither of them said anything, and Sarah felt the room grow a little colder. She was about to rise to turn up the heat, feeling not just chilly but uncomfortable with doing nothing, when Jessica spoke.

"I want to … to say something to you," she started, nervously wringing her hands in her lap, and Sarah's back straightened, anxious now.

"What happened?" she whispered.

"I-I don't know where to start," replied the older woman.

Now Sarah was both nervous *and* curious. "Don't worry," she reassured John's mother. "You can tell me anything."

Jessica let out a troubled sigh and nodded. "John has a past."

At those words, Sarah felt a shiver run down her spine, and it wasn't from the coldness of the room any longer. *John has … a past? What kind of past?*

"I don't know how much he shared with you about it," continued Jessica, rambling on now, "but the girl's name was Kate and she broke his heart. They were in a long time relationship, and things were very serious, but she decided in the end that she wanted to pursue her modelling career over her relationship with my son." There was a bitterness contained within Jessica's words, but she trudged onwards. "John was so upset afterwards, and he ... he turned to drugs and alcohol —he became addicted." She drew in her trembling breath. "I can't forget how lost he became at that time. I helped him recover with much struggling, addiction meetings, and

hospital visits." She paused. "Did you know anything about this, Sarah?"

Sarah didn't reply at first. She could only stare at Jessica with wide eyes, unable to answer or even breathe. John ... her John ... was addicted to alcohol and drugs! He had been in a serious relationship with another woman whom Sarah didn't even know about! She had told John all about her past, including her failed relationships, but John had never once mentioned Kate—or the addiction problems! She sucked in her breath. The first night they had made love, John had gotten drunk on the wine—wine she had given him! Was this her fault now? Was Jessica here because John had become addicted to alcohol again?

"I ... I didn't know any of that," said Sarah, her voice hollow. "He never shared any of it to me."

Jessica gave the other woman a sympathetic look. "Sarah, I really like you, but I'm worried about my son. I've noticed a change in his behaviour. I also know that he is crazily in love with you, but ..." She shook her head. "If he faced such a situation again, I don't know if I would be able to recover him like before."

"I would never do that to him," whispered Sarah, her eyes watering. "I love him."

Jessica gave a soft, yet sad, smile. "Kate said much the same. No one knows what will happen over time. You may be given opportunities that take you overseas —or you may have to move entirely to another state. John ... my son ... is ruining his career already, and this relationship seems to be the cause of his problems."

Sarah simply stared. John was ruining his career? It was the first she had heard of it. Was he skipping work?

"I can't see him like this anymore," said Jessica, pain written across her face. "I'm not against this relationship, because I can see the love you both have for one another, but as his mother, I beg you to keep your distance from John. If you truly love him, you would do this for him." Her eyes were begging. "Promise me, you'll stay away from John so that he may continue on with his career."

Stay away from John? Sarah stared—in shock—at Jessica, unable to say anything. How could she stay away from the man she loved? It seemed ridiculous, but—at the same time—it seemed sensible. If John truly was ruining his career because of her, then perhaps ... perhaps it was for the best.

No, thought Sarah, tears threatening to emerge from her eyes, *no, it is not for the best, but I will do*

SANTONU DHAR

*it anyway, because I love him and I want him to have
everything in life.*

"Okay," she tonelessly agreed.

❊ ❊ ❊

"Damn it, Sarah. Where are you?"

John was sitting in his office at work, constantly
dialing his girlfriend's number but constantly getting
a recorded message about how she wasn't there to
take the call. After being chewed out by Michael for
not being at the earlier meeting, John figured he
would find some comfort in hearing Sarah's voice, but
she seemed not to be near her cell phone. He knew she
wasn't at work, so she must have been out somewhere
with her phone stuffed within her purse, set to low
volume or on silent mode.

Sarah, he thought, a little saddened, *why won't you
answer my calls?*

❊ ❊ ❊

John's face flashed upon Sarah's cell screen once
more and once more she ignored the call. There were
a total of twelve missed calls now, all piling up in
the corner of the screen, reminding Sarah about the
conversation she had had with Jessica earlier today.
It's for the best, she had to tell herself, but that didn't

stop the crying. She felt she would never stop crying.

I'm sorry, John. Sarah placed the phone on the night table and looked away from it, rubbing another batch of tears from her cheeks. *I can't talk to you.*

❅ ❅ ❅

If Sarah won't answer her phone, then I'll just swing by her house, thought John to himself. He abandoned work for the second day in a row, feeling oddly unconcerned about leaving, and grabbed the bus that stopped not far from Sarah's home, having left his car behind to walk today, a decision he now regretted. She still wasn't answering his calls, and now he knew something was up.

❅ ❅ ❅

The doorbell rang, a sound Sarah admittedly hated now, and she grudgingly left her place on the couch to see who it was. She had a feeling she knew who it was, but she had to check anyway, just in case it wasn't *him.*

"Sarah? It's me, Sarah." John's voice was on the other side of the door, and so her suspicions were indeed right. "Please, open the door."

The doorbell rang once, twice, three more times, though Sarah ignored it. She couldn't open the door, not even for him, *especially* not for him.

"Honey," continued John, "please open the door."

Sarah turned away from the door and pressed her back up against it. Suddenly she couldn't control the sadness that had been swelling up inside of her all day, and she began to quietly cry.

"Sarah? I can hear you." John's voice was full of alarm now, and a sense of desperation. "Sarah, tell me what happened. Please open the door and talk to me!"

He sighed in frustration when the door didn't swing open, and Sarah knew he was confused about why she wouldn't see or talk to him, but she couldn't face him about it—not yet.

Heavy footfalls on the porch steps told Sarah that John had left—perhaps in anger considering how hard he had been stomping away—and she slowly pulled open the door, peering down the driveway.

"I'm so sorry, John," she whispered to the empty air, her eyes watering again. She was not pleased with her actions, but she didn't have the strength to speak with him. *I have no other option. I can't see you anymore, so I have to keep my distance. I don't want to waste your life—your dreams. Please ... forgive me, John.*

❊ ❊ ❊

His bed felt harder than usual, though John

figured he was only imagining it. He knew he wouldn't get any

sleep tonight, not while Sarah was ignoring him. *Why, Sarah?* he thought in dismay. *Why are you behaving like this? You know how much I love you ... and I believe you love me as much, so why are you avoiding me?*

John reached into his pocket and drew out his cell phone, once more dialing Sarah's number. Again he was hit by the automatic voice that told him Sarah was away. He wanted to throw his phone across the room, to smash it as the grating voice filled his ears. Why was she doing this to him? Why not speak to him? It was maddening! In desperation, he grabbed his coat from his desk chair and left the room, heading to where comfort called.

It had been a long time since John had been to a place like this. The dark atmosphere and dingy lights made him feel slightly uneasy, and the chattering crowd about the tables and bar did nothing to ease his mind. There were female dancers about, and John shifted his eyes to the barkeep, feeling as though he was betraying Sarah to even look upon them. He ordered a whiskey and sat at the bar, sipping the drink quietly.

After several glasses, John's senses began to slip,

and he angrily wondered why he even cared if Sarah should know he was here. *She* was ignoring *him*. His eyes travelled back to the dancers, allowing their forms to fill his gaze, though in the back of his mind their faces shifted to that of his beloved and he silently swore, downing another glass of liquor.

He felt exhausted, and he knew what he was doing wasn't going to help. But—at the moment—he didn't

even care. *Let Sarah be angry. I'm angry, too*, he thought glumly.

❊ ❊ ❊

Jessica couldn't remember the last time she had been this worried. Her gaze shifted to the clock on the wall to see that it was well past midnight, and John hadn't returned home yet. She knew he couldn't possibly be working this late, and she also knew he wasn't at Sarah's house. He was free to go off and enjoy his time as he pleased, of course, but because of everything that had happened this week, Jessica didn't trust that he was somewhere any good, and *that* was what bothered her.

There was a strange noise at the door, and Jessica's attention was drawn there. It sounded like something was scratching the doorknob, and she jumped from the couch, alarmed. Was someone trying to break in?

Though, the door opened and John stumbled in,

his keys dangling in his hand. He looked completely miserable, and Jessica's heart raced at the sight of him. She could smell the booze from where she stood, could see his drunkenness upon his face. It filled her with horrible memories.

"John," she whispered, voice trembling. "John, are you drunk?"

She knew he was, but somehow asking for confirmation was necessary.

"Yes, mom," grunted John, a little incoherent. "Drunk, drunk, drunk."

John wobbled towards the stairway, and for a moment Jessica only watched him, overcome by grief at the sight of her son. She then quietly moved to his side and helped him upstairs to his room, where he collapsed onto his bed. She returned to the hallway, feeling a little helpless at the state of him.

What happened to my son? She thought miserably. *Did he do that for Sarah? Did I make the wrong decision?*

She peered back inside her son's room. He was sleeping soundlessly, his face at peace, and she smiled at the sight, though it quickly turned into a frown, knowing that this peace would not last and that she had to fix it somehow.

CHAPTER 9

William always enjoyed his days more when Sarah was keeping him company, though he didn't particularly like it when she looked as glum as she did today. His lovely friend was peering out the car window, her chin resting in her hand, a forlorn look within her beautiful eyes. He knew he shouldn't be thinking that way about her, as she was in love with John and would never be with him, but sometimes he couldn't help it. Right now, however, his thoughts were not filled with the things he most loved about Sarah, but concern towards her unhappiness.

"Are you upset, Sarah?" he asked her. She had been mostly quiet the entire car ride, only speaking when he asked her a question. It deeply troubled him.

"Not a bit," she replied, smiling at her friend. It was a lie, William knew, because he recognized that lying smile of hers. She always tried to hide her feelings, and right now he knew she was hurting inside. Though, she didn't seem like she wanted to talk about it just yet, so he didn't press her about it.

Instead, William said, "Good."

He then pulled his car up to the restaurant and parked. It had been a while since they ate out together, but this was their favorite place to go.

Inside, they chose their usual table and ordered their meals. William couldn't help but gaze at Sarah occasionally, still worried about the unhappiness in her eyes. He wondered what she could possibly be upset about. He thought things with John were going well, and there was nothing wrong at work—as far as he knew, anyway. So what could possibly be bothering her?

The waiter brought their food and William dug into his meal, starving from being contained in court all day. Sometimes being a lawyer really sucked, though the pay was fantastic and he couldn't help but love the thrill of closing a case.

"Everything okay?" he chose to ask, but only after he saw that Sarah had barely touched her food. She had ordered her favourite at this place, though she had only taken a few bites, which was not at all like her.

Sarah gave a soft smile as she looked towards him, but there was something false about it, some glimmer of sadness in her eyes. "Yeah, I'm okay."

William placed down his fork and wiped his mouth with a napkin. He had to figure out what was bothering her. He couldn't just leave it at that. He was her friend and he hated seeing her suffer like this. Some part of him believed that her suffering was caused by John, and anger bubbled inside of him

"Sarah, can I say something to you?" he enquired, knowing that he very well might be yelled at for saying anything bad about her beloved.

Though, Sarah didn't seem to hear him. She was staring at her glass, twisting it around on the table.

"Hey, Sarah," said William, a little sharply.

"W-what?" Sarah looked up, a faint blush overcoming her face. William didn't say anything. He simply stared at her, still confused as to why she was so lost. It wasn't like her at all. "Sorry, Bill," she murmured, returning her sad gaze to the glass. "I'm not feeling well today. Can you bring me home? I don't want to stay here any longer."

"Okay," agreed William softly. He paid both bills without Sarah's approval and even helped her into her coat. She didn't seem to notice that, either. Her mind was still lost in thought when they headed across the parking lot towards the car, and she almost tried to open the door of another vehicle.

It isn't good, thought William to himself, as he slipped into the driver's seat. *It isn't good at all.*

❊ ❊ ❊

Trying to read a novel while other thoughts plagued your mind seemed to Sarah to be the worst thing in the world. She could barely concentrate, and she kept skipping ahead, only reading the parts that contained action or major story-progressing moments. Even then, excitement from this once exciting book seemed to slip from her grasp. She eventually tossed it aside, frustrated with it, and takes out her cell phone.

No new emails, but … a missed call from John. Sarah stared at the screen for a while, taking in his name, tasting it on her tongue. She missed saying his name aloud, and she missed hearing his voice. But neither of those things could be in her life.

With a few heavy sobs, Sarah selected his number and blocked it from her list.

❋ ❋ ❋

Things had been a little tense around the apartment lately, and Jessica anxiously made extra food this morning. She had selected John's favorite breakfast food and cooked that, hoping to spark some life within her son. She set his plate down on the table and waited patiently

for him to come downstairs, but when he did he ventured past the kitchen towards the front door.

"John!" called Jessica, rushing to the edge of the kitchen to see him. "Where are you going?"

There was no answer from him. He glared at the door as he swung it open and it slammed loudly behind him. Jessica recoiled, as if he had slapped her in the face, and shakily took a seat at the table. A sob overtook her and she cried into the hem of her dress, knowing that the past was about to repeat itself.

* * *

Another day, another case to close, thought Sarah glumly, as she peered into the mirror. Her suit had been ironed the day before—remembering to do it this time—and she was dressed for work, ready to head to the courthouse. She paused at the front door to grab her briefcase and coat and then swung it open, only halting when she saw someone standing outside. The sight of someone standing on her porch had made her jump, and her heart trembled slightly, knowing that she would not have been able to handle herself if it had been John standing out there, but it was Jessica, and Sarah had to mentally keep all of her bubbling emotions contained.

She was angry at the woman. This torture ... it was Jessica's fault, even if it was for the best, it was *still* her fault. And Sarah had tried very hard not to be bitter about it all, but eventually she gave into her feelings and allowed herself to be angry.

"Please, come in," she said tartly.

Jessica didn't look at her when she entered the house and moved towards the living room to have a seat. Sarah

sat a short distance away from the older woman, dropping her briefcase to the side of the couch. She had a few minutes to spare, since she had woken up a little early today, unable to sleep because of all the nightmares she had been having, reliving losing John over and over again.

"I am ... *so* sorry, Sarah," whispered Jessica, finally able to meet Sarah's gaze.

Sarah said nothing to this. Why was this woman apologizing? Did something happen to John?

"Please, forgive me, Sarah," pleaded Jessica, reaching out to take Sarah's hands. The latter felt her muscles tense, not wanting to be touched by this woman. "Forgive me, Sarah," continued Jessica, speaking very softly now. "I beg my apologies. I was wrong to drive you from John! I see that now. You have become a part of his life." There were tears in her eyes, though Sarah chose not to forgive her just yet. She was still bitter. "I was concerned that your relationship was diverting him from his goals, but I was completely wrong. Whatever John is doing, he is doing it to himself, and he is worse without you."

Sarah started. She felt her fingers clench around Jessica's hands. It wasn't her that was affecting John.

"I can't see him in pain anymore," whimpered

Jessica, crying now. "Please, you must come back into his life. *Please* ..."

Sarah couldn't control herself any longer. She cried aloud and nodded fiercely, agreeing that she would go back to John. She murmured her forgiveness to what Jessica had done and the older woman became relieved, kissing the young lady upon the forehead.

"Jessica, tell me what happened," pleaded Sarah, her grip upon the other's hands firm now. "Tell me about John."

❋ ❋ ❋

John hadn't felt much in the mood to drink tonight, though he had managed to get a few shots in him. He think he was developing the flu or something, so he didn't want to make matters worse by consuming too much alcohol, but still ... a few drinks felt good in him.

He had reached his apartment and he found his key in his pocket, wondering if he was to scratch up the lock again like last time, though he found he wasn't that drunk this time and fit the key snugly into the lock. He paused, however, hearing voices from inside. He shrugged it off and pushed open the door, only to see Sarah sitting on the couch with his mother. His heart instantly did a flip, a cold sweat washing down over him. John figured the television had been on, or his mother was talking on the phone with someone. Never Sarah!

But there she was, rising from her spot on the couch, and John became lightheaded. Did he look drunk? Was his clothes messed up? Did he smell terrible from the alcohol?

"Sarah," he mumbled out, pushing aside his fears. "It's you."

"Yes, Honey," she said, smiling a little. She abruptly hugged him, and John just stood there, not moving his arms, overwhelmed by her actions. He was still staring at her when she moved away, completely shocked.

"Sarah ... what's going on?" He looked between her and his mother, but neither said anything to answer his question.

His mother simply smiled, though it was filled with sadness. "John, forgive your mother. It was my fault all of this has happened."

"I don't understand," John blurted out, still overly confused.

"I'll explain everything later," said Jessica. She pulled on her coat and moved towards the door. "I'm going out for a little while and you two can talk."

She then left and John turned to Sarah, searching for some explanation.

"I'm sorry for everything," she whispered,

touching his face.

You're sorry? John shook his head. "Sarah … I've … I've been acting like a fool this past week and—"

She pressed a finger to his lips and gave him a troubled look. "We've both been fools, John. Let's just forget about all of this and move on. I don't want to be without you again."

"Sarah …" John smiled softly and kissed her cheek, relief bubbling up inside. They were starting fresh again, and John knew he would need some time to let go of the things he had grown accustomed to over the past week. But with Sarah by his side, he was sure he would get back to his normal life in no time at all.

Outside, the rain was falling harshly against the earth. Sarah lifted her mug of coffee to her lips and inhaled the aroma before taking a sip. It was the perfect addition to a day like this. Rainy days were always full of loneliness,

or so it seemed that way to Sarah. She watched the rain against the tops of cars as they sped by and encircled both hands around her mug, feeling for its warmth.

John was back in her life now. Everything was good again. She loved him with all of her soul and being. Every second she lived, she felt she lived it for him. She could taste his name on her breath, could inhale his scent when he wasn't near. Every moment she spent was spent in anticipation to be with him forever. She felt that—without him—her life would be meaningless, for she had placed him within her future, and if was not there to spend that future with her, her happiness would dissolve into nothingness.

A figure was running up the driveway, and Sarah smiled and headed towards the door. She didn't wait for it to ring. She pulled it open and ushered John inside. His hair was damp and hung around his forehead in dipping strands, and his coat was soaked through. Sarah fetched a towel from the bathroom and gave it to him, before disappearing into the kitchen to make him a cup of hot coffee.

John hung his jacket on the coat rack, away from the other, dry garments and sat on the couch. Sarah returned with his coffee and he sipped it with appreciation, allowing the mug to warm his cold hands.

"I'm going on a trip to India soon," he remarked, once Sarah had taken a seat.

"India?" repeated Sarah, surprised.

"Yeah, I have a close friend who lives there— Akash," John added, giving her the name.

Sarah smiled slyly. "Are you telling me so far in advance because you want me to go with you?"

John returned the smile. "Maybe. Do you want to go?"

"Sure!" Sarah relaxed back in her chair and crossed her legs. "When were you planning on leaving?"

John placed his mug on the coffee table, empty now. "Sometime next week. I'll make the arrangements. You just pick what you want to pack and bring your beautiful smile."

Sarah then gave him one of those alleged beautiful smiles. "Okay."

***

The television was on again, and Sarah was once more looking for a good show to watch. It seemed like a constant routine, but it was the middle of the year and most shows were off for the season. She eventually muted the volume and picked up her phone, remembering something very important. She had already put a notice in for a leave of absence at work, but she had clients to deal with while she was gone. In the past, William had been fine with handling any work she needed done while out of town, and—in return—she had helped him out when he wasn't feeling well. So she figured he wouldn't mind helping her out again. Besides, best friends were always there for one another.

Sarah dialed his number and lifted the phone to her ear, waiting for him to answer.

❊ ❊ ❊

William sighed and tossed another pen in the trash bin. He really should have just went for the expensive brand and not bothered with the cheap stuff, but he had been in a hurry and late to get in, so it was a quick

decision on his part. Quick, yet horrible. He fished another pen out of his desk and got back to writing up a report, pleased to see that this pen was working.

His office was well furnished and decorated with a variety of plants, pictures, and books. He even had a few gadgets on his desk, one of which clicked back and forth, a sound he had grown accustomed to. It helped him focus, especially when obnoxious pens kept failing for him.

The cell on his desk vibrated nosily, startling him, and William reached over to pick it up, even more surprised when it was Sarah calling him. She never called when he was at work, though she probably was still out of sorts, like she had been at the restaurant, and was just calling to hear a familiar voice.

"Hello, Sarah," said William softly, answering the call. "How are you?"

"I'm fine!" William started at the voice on the other line. There was no sadness to it now, just the cheerful, familiar tone he was used to hearing from the woman. "I actually have a request for you. I'm planning on going on vacation for a week, so I won't be in the office. Do you mind handling my work while I'm away?"

William wrinkled his brow. "Vacation?" he said, ignoring her request for a moment. "Where are you going?"

"Oh, John and I are going to India?" He could hear her excitement on the other end, and he found himself hating that he hated how happy she was.

"Oh ..." he murmured. He was hoping the situation between those two had worsened, and Sarah was calling to tell him that she was over John, but it seemed it was in fact the opposite.

"Bill?" Sarah's voice came to his ears. "Bill, are you still there?"

"Yes." William rubbed his forehead. "I'll manage things while you're away."

"Thanks so much, buddy!" said Sarah cheerfully. "You're so helpful! And, Bill—" She paused for a moment, her voice lowering. "I'm really sorry I was so out of it before. You were trying to help me out and I pushed you away. Forgive me?"

"Sure," said William. How could he ever be mad at her?

"So, now that we're talking, how is everything going for you lately?" asked Sarah conversationally.

"It's going ... good." William cleared his throat and

looked down at his paperwork. "I'd love to talk more but I have a lot of things to get done here. Another time, Sarah?"

"Of course! I have to pack anyway," she said, excited again now. "Be in touch soon! Thanks again, Bill!"

"It's my pleasure," murmured William into the phone. "Take care."

"You, too!"

He ended the call and flicked his phone onto the desk, annoyed at it. His paperwork suddenly didn't seem as important to him as it had moments ago. Sarah was no longer upset because of John, and everything was good.

William suddenly felt that the only chance to have Sarah had been abruptly taken away from him.

CHAPTER 10

Turbulence jolted Sarah awake, and she sat upright in her chair, a little dazed. John was sitting next to her, amused by the expression upon her face, and she smiled meekly, wondering if she had been drooling or doing something equally embarrassing. A pile of magazines rested nearby, and John—seeing the word 'technology' splashed upon some—reached to grab one. They were in first class and the seats had been so comfy that Sarah had found herself asleep soon after takeoff. Now she was feeling rather tired again, even after her nap, and she laid her head against John's shoulder, ready to settle down for another.

John gazed down at her, smiling warmly. He wrapped his free arm around her.

❋ ❋ ❋

The Delhi airport was huge, but John managed to navigate his way through the crowd, his hand locked around Sarah's, making sure they didn't get separated in the mess of people. The speaker overhead was warning that another plane was about to depart, while another had arrived. John searched the crowds, eager to find his friend, and soon spotted him.

Akash was standing close to the exit, sporting a button-down shirt and dark pants with a pair of black sunglasses. He grinned when he saw John approach and the two embraced. When they moved out of the hug, John extended his hand to Sarah.

"Akash, this is Sarah," he introduced.

"Hi, Sarah," said Akash, taking her hand in both of his and shaking it. "I'm Akash. I've heard so much about you."

Sarah blushed. "Hello, Akash. It's a pleasure to meet you."

"John." Akash turned to his friend. "My car is parked just outside. Please, follow me."

John wheeled his luggage bag outside, tagging along after his friend. Akash led them to his vehicle, a new model of the Mitsubishi Pajero, and the two Americans loaded their things in the trunk.

"How is everything going?" asked John conversationally, as they all piled into the SUV.

"Everything's good," replied Akash, as he started the vehicle. "What about you?"

"I've just started a business," said John proudly, and he explained the firm where he worked with his partner, Michael.

Akash listened intently to this and nodded as John finished. "That all sounds really great, my friend." He laughed and shifted his gaze back to Sarah for a moment. "John and I have remained great friends since graduating from Harvard. I decided to come to India while he moved to New York. It's been a long time since we last saw each other."

"Yes, it has," agreed John. "You told me yesterday that you were married."

"Yes!" exclaimed Akash, throwing his friend a bright smile. "I was married three months ago. Nidhi and I were dating for two years, and I thought it was about time to ask for her hand. I'm sorry I didn't mention it before now, but it just happened so fast!" He grimaced. "Our families were against the relationship, so we had to elope."

John's expression contorted. "Sorry about your family, but at least everything worked out in the end."

"True," agreed Akash. He inclined his head forward. "That's our apartment over there. Let's continue the conversation inside. I can't wait for you to meet Nidhi."

Akash parked his vehicle and John unloaded the luggage from the back. Sarah took her bag and extended the handle to allow the luggage to roll behind her. The three of them approached the door and Akash pressed the call button. A beautiful young woman wearing a brightly colored saree opened the door, her dark hair braided over her shoulder. She smiled when she saw Akash and moved aside to let everyone in.

"Nidhi, this is my best friend, John. I told you about him, remember?" Akash pointed to the other young lady. "And this is Sarah, John's girlfriend."

"Namaste," said Sarah.

Nidhi looked surprised. "Oh, do you know Hindi?"

Sarah laughed and blushed. "Well, just that one word."

Nidhi laughed as well. "Oh, I see. How was the trip here?"

"We enjoyed it," answered John. "It didn't take long at all."

Akash scowled at the window. "You're lucky there wasn't much traffic today. Usually you'd have to wait more than an hour at the traffic lights."

John blinked in surprise. "Really? Wow, that's rough."

"Yeah, it's really frustrating here sometimes," said Akash with a shake of his head.

✽ ✽ ✽

The evening had passed rather quickly and Sarah was in the living room of the young Indian couple's apartment, allowing Nidhi to teach her how to drape a blue seree around her body. Sarah had wanted to try it herself after being shown how to do it, but she quickly became frustrated with the piece of cloth after it got tangled into a mess again.

"God!" she swore, bundling it up and tossing it on the couch. "It's so difficult to drape a seree, Nidhi!"

Nidhi laughed at the other woman's tactics. "Managing it is tougher."

"Oh my god …" Sarah fell onto the couch. "How do you do it?"

Nidhi shrugged. "It comes with practice." She pointed to the saree and Sarah sighed as she grabbed it and stood up. "You'll learn soon if you don't give up."

"Thanks, Nidhi," said Sarah, studying the fabric in her hands. "I do want John to see me in this."

"I bet it will look stunning on you." Nidhi winked. "Your man won't be able to keep his eyes off of you."

Sarah blushed and shrugged off the comment. "If I put it on right, he won't, but if I wear it wrong he'll just tease."

"And that's why you have me to help you," said Nidhi with a smile, and she took the saree from Sarah's hands.

John had not seen Sarah for what seemed like all day. Akash had left for bed shortly ago and now John was sitting alone in the living room of the apartment, reading a novel he had brought from home. He figured Nidhi had taken his girlfriend around the neighbourhood, perhaps

shown her a few sights. He was a little jealous at the thought of it, as he had spent most of the day speaking with Akash in the back area of the apartment building, admiring the view from there. Sarah wouldn't *really* go exploring without him, though ... right?

A hand touched his shoulder and moved across his neck and John glanced up in surprise to see Sarah coming around the chair. In the dim light of the living room, the shadows seemed to move up and down her pale reflection, causing her hair to become alive with color. She was wearing a blue saree, and in the dark room she appeared to him to be a foreign goddess, masked in the garments of another culture.

John rose from the chair, unable to speak, and touched her neck lightly, wondering if he was in some sort of strange dream. She was real enough, and so he kissed where he touched, feeling the warm skin under his lips. He held her close, wanting to lose himself within her, and she moved away, a sly smile upon her face. The strange creature led him towards the bedroom with her slender hand, and he followed eagerly, desiring every touch and kiss she was able to give.

The door shut and they fell onto the bed. John traced Sarah's lips with his thumb, and she smiled against it, beckoning him forward. He kissed her, fervently and without delay. Her body seemed moved in time with his own, and her lips returned his kisses with just as much passion.

In the pounding darkness, John lost himself in her ardent love.

***

There really wasn't much sense in reading the newspaper when you couldn't understand a word of it, but John searched through for comics or word puzzles, trying to find at least that to fix his need of having a newspaper in the morning. He somewhat understand what was going on in this part of world from the pictures, but everything else was a mystery.

Thankfully, a knock came at the door and John put down the paper, eager to get the day started. Akash came in with two white garments in his hands and placed them at the foot of the bed.

"What do you have there?" questioned John, peering down at the clothes.

"This one is called a kurta," replied Akash, pointing to the one on the left, "and the other is a payjama."

"I see," murmured John. He looked back up to his friend. "Is there a festival today?"

"There sure is!" Akash laughed. "And you're going to be wearing these. Today we're celebrating Holi!"

"Holi?" John swung his legs out onto the floor. "I've never heard of it."

"Holi is the festival of colors," explained Akash, as he moved towards the door. "It brings with it the utmost joy and warmth, the spirit of togetherness … and it starts soon."

John nodded. "Wow—I'll be ready in about five minutes."

"Okay. Hurry up!" Akash shut the door behind him.

The festival that brings joy and warmth, thought John considerately. The image of Sarah flashed through his mind and he smiled at the clothes on his bed.

❊ ❊ ❊

Lights were strung everywhere, with music playing somewhere nearby and a swarm of people in brightly-colored clothing filling the streets. John found it hard to concentrate with all the paint and laughter, but he somehow managed to stick with his group and maneuver through the crowd. Every once in a while he was hit with a burst of colored powder from somewhere, or his feet were splashed by the bursting of a water balloon. At first he hoped that Akash wouldn't mind him getting his clothes all dirty, but he quickly realized that a fun part of the festival was to muddy up your clothes with the provided amusements.

John was just asking Akash where they should go next when two hands clapped around his face and a cloud of purple powder floated out before him. He coughed and didn't have time to run away before there were purple spots on his white clothes, too. Sarah was standing nearby, bending over laughing from her little trick, and John saw that Akash hadn't escaped his wife's attack, either. Though, Akash grabbed a handful of green powder and dashed after the women. They ran—like their very lives depended upon it—and John chuckled and scooped up a pile of yellow powder.

Luckily, the men were faster on their feet, and the crowd slowed the women down considerably, so they were caught in no time at all, John and Akash taking revenge upon them. The girls retaliated with some close-by water balloons, and another round had started.

❊ ❊ ❊

Later that night, the four were in the kitchen, John and Sarah happily chatting away to the young Indian couple about the great day they had been a part of. Nidhi served a few rice dishes and sat next to her husband, a little bit of powder still in her dark hair from the earlier fights. Sarah dug into her foot instantly, starving from the day's activities and complimented Nidhi on the food, nodding her approval. John was certain his girlfriend would eat just about anything when she was hungry, though he didn't say that aloud, fearing both women would take offense to the comment. He chuckled at the thought, received a curious look from Sarah, and then cleared his throat.

"So, Akash, how's your business going?" he asked quickly.

"Everything's good!" replied Akash. "I expect to get a big project from the Indian government soon."

"Really?" said John, surprised. "That's fantastic."

"I want to involve you in this project, as well," continued Akash, pointing his fork towards John. "What do you say?"

"I'm flattered," said John, even more surprised. "How would I be involved?"

"I'll discuss the details with you later—"

Nidhi sighed in annoyance and gave her husband an exasperated look. "Oh, no more business topics, Akash! It's a holiday!"

Akash gave his wife an apologetic smile. "Sorry, no

more business discussion. I promise." He turned back to John and Sarah. "Guess what? We're going to visit the great Taj Mahal tomorrow."

Finally! John thought to himself. *Something I've heard of!* "I'm very excited to visit Taj Mahal. I've heard and read so much about it, so I was looking forward to seeing it on this trip."

Sarah leaned on her elbow. "Well, I haven't heard of it, so it's all new to me. What other exciting plans do you have for us, Akash?" she asked curiously.

"Of course!" Akash smiled. "After visiting Taj Mahal, we're going to take a trip to Goa directly from Agra."

John furrowed his eyebrow and crossed his arms. "Goa?"

"Yes, it's a beach along the sea," explained Akash.

Nidhi clapped her hands together once in excitement. "Wow! That's a great idea!"

"Yeah! A beach would be a great escape from the heat." Sarah looked up to John. "What do you think?" She stared at him for a moment, and when he didn't answer, she said, "John? Sarah to John, are you listening?"

John laughed quietly and nodded. "Yes," he said softly. "I think Goa is a fantastic idea."

Akash leaned back in his chair, done eating. "I have another purpose to go to Goa."

"Oh?" John looked up from the table he had been admiring in thought.

"It's been three months since our wedding," started Akash, looking at Nidhi, "and we haven't taken our honeymoon yet. Goa seems like the perfect place for it."

Nidhi laughed into her hand and blushed. "Thank you. Finally you've got some time for it."

"But our time is almost up here," commented John, as he gazed at Sarah. He turned back to Akash. "Sarah and I need to get back to New York after tomorrow. We'll join you for a day at Goa."

"Okay," said Akash. "You can catch a flight back straight from Goa. It should be no problem at all."

Nidhi glanced nervously to her husband. "Have you made any arrangements for the trip?"

Akash offered his wife and soft smile and placed an arm around her shoulder. "Don't worry, my love. I've made those arrangements already, and I'll book tickets from Goa to New York for them online tonight." He looked back to John and Sarah. "Just make sure you have everything packed and brought with you to Goa."

John gave his friend a grateful smile. "Thanks, Akash. That would be great."

They discussed the trip to Goa a little more, Sarah excited to go to a beach, and then they finished their dinner and headed to their rooms, ready for bed. John watched as Sarah rambled on for another hour about the trip, until he hushed her up with kisses. She fell asleep soon afterwards, tired from the adventure they had gone on today, and John lay awake in bed for a little while, thinking about tomorrow.

Goa, he thought, *was going to be one trip to remember*.

CHAPTER 11

They left early for their trip to the mausoleum, Taj Mahal. Akash took his Pajero and parked as close to the entrance as he could manage. It was busy at the mausoleum today, though Sarah figured it was likely to be busy every day as it was a tourist attraction. They went in through the front entrance and Akash began them on a tour of the place. Sarah snapped as many pictures as she could. She had promised herself to get lots to bring home so she could get one of those giant photo albums and fill it up. She had never been on a trip like this before, and so pictures were essential. They would be memories of her first vacation with John.

"This is amazing!" exclaimed Sarah, as she took a random photo of the above architecture. The amount of detail baffled her. She hadn't been in such a grand place before.

"It is," agreed John, peering up at the ceiling. "It is regarded as one of the eight wonders of the world. Like I said last night, I've been waiting a while to see this place, and now that I'm here … well, it was worth the wait."

Nidhi tapped Sarah on the shoulder and she lowered her camera. "Did you know that it was constructed by a Muslim emperor named Shah Jahan in memory of his dear wife, Queen Mumtaz?"

Sarah shook her head. "I don't really know anything about this place, but I'd sure like to know more."

It was Akash's turn to impress the American couple. "Taj Mahal was built over a period of twenty years. More than twenty-thousand workers were appointed to complete this monument and it was completed at the cost of thirty-two million rupees."

"Wow." John was baffled. "That much? Really?"

"Yeah." Akash took a look around as they moved to the next area of the mausoleum. "It's unbelievable. For a seventeenth century monument, it's marvellous!"

"I'm really impressed with the architecture here," commented Sarah, as she snapped another shot of a random wall. John was sure most of the pictures would be like that: random photos of random things, maybe a shot with someone's body with no head, a picture of a sign with half the words missing.

John linked his arm with Sarah's. "Me too," he agreed, grinning.

* * *

Outside, the mausoleum was just as grand, and

John took Sarah along the outer walls to stare at the beauty of the structure with him. She had put her camera in her bag for now, deciding to save some space for their trip to Goa, and was admiring Taj Mahal within a beautiful courtyard. She was breathtaking as usual, today, but somehow her excitement gave her a more radiant look, and John found himself unable to keep his well-kept secret a secret any longer. He had meant to save this moment for Goa, but the chances of making it to Goa without spilling the secret was slim at best.

Reaching into his jacket pocket, John pulled out the tiny black box and moved around to face Sarah. She had a strange expression on her face, like that of someone who wanted to ask why he had suddenly jumped in front of her, blocking her view of the mausoleum, and who also knew something was about to happen.

John knelt down onto one knee and opened the box. Inside was a diamond ring—an expensive one that he knew Sarah would love—and he had purchased it shortly before the trip, knowing that this trip would be the perfect opportunity to propose to his beloved. He hadn't just mentioned the trip to her in hopes that she had wanted to go with him; he had asked specifically so that she would come here and he could pop the big question.

"I wanted to wait until we were in Goa, but I couldn't resist temptation any longer," said John in a rush. The expression on Sarah's face, a mix of surprise and eagerness, melted away his nervousness and replaced it with love. *This is the woman I want to marry*, he thought keenly. He knew it from the first time he had seen her: sitting lovely at the bus stop reading a newspaper. She was beautiful, talented, intelligent and witty—everything a woman could be and more. He had known for a long time that she had to be the one, and now he would make her his if she agreed to it.

"Since this is a lovely place and we are amidst a lovely moment, I thought I would ask you now." He pulled the ring from the box and offered it to her, the gem glinting in the early sunlight. "Miss Sarah Jane Miller, will you marry me?"

Sarah folded both hands over her mouth, hiding the wide grin that had exploded across her lips. "Why yes, Mister Deane, I will marry you," she said, her voice high with amusement and slightly breathless.

John barely got the ring on her finger before she leapt into his arms, nearly knocking him off his feet. He laughed and spun her around before placing her back on the ground, though she didn't let go of him. He wanted to kiss her—like they had passionately kissed the night she

had snuck up on him wearing that seree—but his friend and wife were approaching now, and they were already shouting out their congratulations to the happy couple. Nidhi hugged Sarah and Akash shook John's hand several times and patted him on the back, both verbally praising them and offering good wishes and happy sentiments to the future.

The four afterwards chatted for a bit in the courtyard, Sarah shifting her eyes from her ring to the others from time to time, and then they left Taj Mahal, heading back to where Akash parked the car.

John didn't let go of Sarah's hand the whole way there.

✽ ✽ ✽

Akash hired a driver to take them to the Agra Airport, as he didn't want to leave his car overnight there. John sat next to Sarah in the backseat, leaning his arm up against the window. The girls were small but the cab was not, and so it was a tight fit. The luggage was secured in the trunk of the car, packed in tighter than Tetris blocks, and John feared the trunk door would pop open any second, vomiting their suitcases out onto the road. He grimaced at the thought.

Nidhi leaned forward in her seat as John continued his worrying.

"How long will it take to reach Goa by plane?" she asked her husband, touching him lightly on the shoulder. She glanced back at John and Sarah, and saw the weary look on their faces. "We are all a little tired."

"Yeah," agreed John, feeling a little sheepish. He

was used to early mornings, but the entire trip so far had been quite the rush and he was feeling a little drained.

Akash leaned around his seat and smiled at the three of them. "Don't worry, everyone. It'll only take a few hours—two or three at the most—and we'll be on the ground and you'll all be energized by the sight of the beach."

John sighed in relief. The first thing he was going to do on the plane was take a nap. In the meantime—

He looked over his shoulder and through the window at the trunk. No lost luggage yet.

❋ ❋ ❋

Now this *is what I call a vacation.* Sarah let her sunglasses fall over her eyes and leaned back on her blanket. The hot sun warmed her skin nicely, and the sand felt good between her toes. Nidhi was lying on a blanket next to her, humming quietly and smiling. The men were out in the water, having a quick swim. Sarah had passed on swimming. Maybe later she would go out there with John and challenge him to a few races, but for now she just wanted to lie back and relax for a while. The Goa Beach was crowded, and she had already been covered in sand by a few kids kicking around a beach ball, so she figured a nice swim would be an end-of-the-day activity. She was also glad she had started working out a few months before her trip

—her bikini fit her nicely, and she was sure John had noticed her light-blue getup.

He looked her way then, and she waved to him, smiling brightly. He returned the gesture, and Akash took that opportunity to splash his friend. Sarah heard him laughing from where she lay, and Nidhi broke out into silent giggles. They were immersed in a water fight now, prancing through the water and trying to push the other under.

The American girl lifted her sunglasses and peered across the beach, spotting a volleyball net not far away. In high school, she had been on the volleyball team. She had even won a few medals. It was a fun sport, and she wouldn't mind having a few rounds of it now. Hopefully she hadn't forgotten how to play.

"John! Akash!" She cupped her hands around her mouth as she called to them, and they hurried in from the ocean, beads of water dripping off their swim trunks. Their feet were dark from the sand that stuck to them, and Sarah rose from her blanket to greet them. "Do you guys want to play volleyball?"

The two men looked to one another. Akash shrugged and John turned back to Sarah, nodding his head in approval. "Yeah, let's give it a try."

Sarah clapped her hands together once in enthusiasm and held out one hand to Nidhi. She took it, and then the two women were running off down the beach towards the net, Nidhi holding on to her sun hat to keep it from flying off. Sarah hadn't felt this young in years! Maybe it was the proposal John had given her earlier. She bit her lip in excitement. Engaged, she was *engaged*! And to the love of her life, no less! She couldn't wait to tell Amanda and her aunt and uncle and William and—

Cut it out, Sarah! she scolded herself. *Get your mind back on the glorious vacation! And the beach hunk.* She winked at John, who smiled sheepishly back. *We're going to be married!*

So maybe the excitement wouldn't control itself *that* easily, but at least now she had something to do that was invigorating and wouldn't allow her mind to drift back to her engagement. As long as she focused on the ball, she would get through the game without being too distracted.

"Who wants first serve?" asked John, as he discovered a ball half buried in the sand. He brushed it off. "And how should we choose teams?"

"Girls versus boys!" shouted Nidhi, laughing and hurrying over to the opposite side of the net where Sarah stood.

"We won't go easy on you!" Akash called back, also laughing now.

"You'll both be coughing up sand when we're done with you!" taunted Sarah, as she caught the ball.

Both John and Akash looked to one another, voicing quiet "ooo's", as if pretending to be frightened by her insult, and then the match began. After a while of fierce competition, the couples eventually forgot about their rivalry and played a few games, but not without slipping in the sand several times and getting tangled up in the net more than once, causing Sarah to wonder if she had just imagined herself to have once been a great volleyball player.

Eventually they grew tired of the game and wound up at the snack bar, where John purchased a bottle of water and some tasty looking chocolates for himself and Sarah. She then grabbed her camera and snatched up John's hand, leading him bouncing down across the sand towards a row of palm trees spread out across the beach.

John snapped a few photos of the area, making sure to grab a snapshot of a hermit crab scurrying to escape the humans and a strangely-colored bird nesting in the trees above. Sarah was busy licking the last of the chocolate off her fingers when John grabbed her wrist and pulled her into a tight embrace. His lips melted over hers, warm and strong in the cool breeze of the ocean. When he pulled away, he was smiling.

"That had to be the most delicious kiss I've ever had," he commented deviously. "I may have to go back and buy more of that chocolate."

Sarah giggled and moved away, watching him slyly from the corner of her eye. He followed her down the beach and into a cluster of palm trees, where she sat against the slim trunk. John joined her, intoxicated by her presence, and sat cross-legged on the sand.

"I'll always remember this trip," said Sarah softly, as she leaned forward towards the sand. She dug her index finger into the yellow grains and began to draw. She spelled out the letters "S" and "J" and formed a heart around them, smiling bashfully as she finished. "And this trip will always remember us now."

John touched her cheek and turned her to face him. She saw the glimmer of happiness in his eyes, and her heart tumbled frantically in her chest. He was so perfect for her, so meant to be hers. Some days she couldn't believe that this was her life. Everything she had ever wanted was hers, and today the man of her dreams had asked her to be his wife.

"You've never looked so alive than you have today, Sarah," said John gently, stroking her cheek with his fingers. "I'm glad you had so much fun."

"I'm glad you invited me." Sarah moved from the sand and onto John's lap, draping her arms gently around his neck. She bent down to seductively whisper into his ear. "I love you."

She felt him kiss her neck gently, slowly. His tongue touched her ear and she shivered against him. Her eyes fell closed and she leaned into him, allowing his body heat to warm her. The moment was perfect ... peaceful. Sarah relaxed in his arms and allowed him to kiss her

neck and along her collarbone. Someday in the future, they would be married, and he would be forever hers. She smiled against his shoulder. *Hers.* It felt so right to think it, to taste it on her tongue and feel it in her every touch. That's how it should be, because they were meant for each other, and Sarah had felt that way ever since she had met him.

A second later, John had pulled out Sarah's camera and she drew her head out of its hiding place against his shoulder to peer up at the square object.

"Smile, sweetheart," whispered John, as he kissed her cheek.

She did smile—perhaps a little too broadly—and the camera flash flickered through her eyes, capturing the moment forever.

CHAPTER 12

The trip to India had been a great distraction from their busy lives in New York, but John and Sarah were now ready to get back home. They were standing in the airport at Goa, waiting for their flight back to the city. Akash and Nidhi had escorted them and kept them company while they waited for their plane to arrive. John was overly pleased with the trip. Not only did he get to spend time with one of his close friends, but he also managed to ask Sarah the question he had been meaning to ask for a while now. He didn't know where he had found the courage for it, but he was glad it was over. He had been worried about it for a while, wondering how she would react. Thankfully she had said yes.

Sarah was hugging Nidhi, a sad smile upon her face, though there was light in her eyes, too, and John knew she was still thinking about their future. She had been distracted all day thinking about it, and every time he glanced her way she was smiling and blushing and fidgeting with something. Truly, she was happy.

"Good bye, Nidhi," said Sarah, pulling away from

the Indian woman. "We had a wonderful time here. I won't forget you."

"Yeah," agreed Nidhi. "Be sure to keep in contact and maybe persuade your fiancé to visit again."

Sarah laughed and shot John a look out of the corner of her eye. "I will do that." There was a faint blush on her cheeks at the mention of the word "fiancé" and John returned Sarah's loving look, contented that she was so pleased.

"Well, I'm not happy," said Akash, after giving John a farewell hug, as well. "I expected you guys to stay longer. The vacation felt like it passed much too quickly for my liking."

John tapped the screen of his phone and gave Akash a sympathetic look. "Unfortunately, my email is bubbling over with work-related messages, so I have to get back before Michael finds himself in too much trouble." He glanced to Sarah. "And my *fiancé* here has to return to court in a few days."

"Well, I hope you visit again after your wedding," said Akash.

"Sure," agreed John, nodding. He placed a hand on Akash's shoulder and looked towards the bordering area. Things were starting to get busy. "I think it's time to go. Take care, my friend. I'll talk to you soon."

Sarah waved to Nidhi as she hurried after John, who was heading quickly towards the plane's gateway.

"I'll call you, Nidhi! Take care of yourself! Bye!"

The young couple waited in the airport until their American friends were safely onboard the plane, and then they left, returning to their long-planned honeymoon.

* * *

The flight ran smoothly, but neither John nor Sarah managed to get any sleep. They were tired from the trip but also spirited, knowing that things were going to be busy when they reached the city. John's head was filled to the brim with work, though there was space inside for thoughts of the wedding, too, and he knew Sarah was excited to plan it all out. He just hoped she wouldn't get

too carried away with it and forget about other important things.

It was a big step in their relationship and John couldn't wait to arrive there. He knew planning a wedding took a lot of work and dedication, but he was determined to get through it and marry the woman of his dreams. No matter what, he would see her walk down the aisle in a white dress.

"Do you see him?" asked Sarah, standing on her toes to get a better view. They were looking for their prearranged driver, but the crowd wasn't helping their search much. The airport was about as full as usual, people stepping on other people's toes.

"Over there." John pointed through a gap in the swarm of people and Sarah slipped her hand into his as they made their way towards the man, not wanting to get separated.

They were led outside and to their car. John pushed their luggage into the trunk and they got inside the black vehicle. The driver started the engine, asked for a destination, and they were off.

"I had such a great time," whispered Sarah, as she leaned her head down upon John's shoulder. She looked extremely tired, her eyes no longer bright and lively. "I'm so glad we're about to experience a new step in our life." She sighed in contentment. "I'll never forget this trip."

"Me neither," agreed John. He slipped his hand into Sarah's and netted their fingers together. Soon rings would adorn their hands, signifying their union and love for one another. It made John giddy.

"Nidhi and Akash make a lovely couple," murmured Sarah, closing her eyes.

John smiled down at her, though she couldn't see it. "They do. We'll miss them."

"Mmhmm," mumbled Sarah. She yawned and covered it with the back of her hand. "I learned a lot from Nidhi about her culture, especially wearing that pesky saree."

John quietly laughed. "You looked beautiful that night." He thought back to when Sarah had snuck up on him from behind, the foreign cloth wrapped around her slim frame. He had thought her to look like some sort of goddess, and it had drove him mad with desire.

"She gave me that one, actually," said Sarah, "and I bought a few more at the market."

"Really?" John raised his eyebrows in amusement. For something so "pesky" Sarah seemed to like it, or maybe she just liked the fact that he enjoyed the way she looked in them.

"Yeah ..." Sarah pushed her head farther into the curve of John's neck, letting her warm breath pour down upon him. "Oh, I also learned some Indian cuisine recipes from her. I'll have to try some out when I get home."

"That sounds fun," commented John. "Can I be your taste-tester?"

Sarah smiled against his shoulder. "Sure. I'll try cooking something the next time you come over for lunch."

"First stop," the driver called back to them, slowing the car.

John glanced out the window to see Sarah's house. "I guess we're here already."

Sarah lifted her head and kissed him on the cheek.

"Why don't you come inside with me? You can go back to your place tomorrow."

John felt the weight of his phone in his pocket and struggled with his decision. He wanted to go inside with her—he really did. He wanted to hold her in his arms and make love to her and then just relish in the fact that soon she would be his wife. "Sorry, sweetheart," he finally said, a little jadedly, knowing that work would have to come first this time. He had a lot to take care of. "I'm going to catch up with Michael tonight and get an early rest."

"Okay," said Sarah, disappointed. She slid out of the car and retrieved her luggage before bending her head down to glance back into the vehicle. "You'll call tonight, though? I'll wait up for you."

"I will. I promise." He placed his hand on the handle of the door. "Now go relax for a bit. I'll talk to you later."

Sarah smiled and turned to go, waving her hand as she did. "Bye, John."

"Take care." John shut the door.

The car started back down the street. The remainder of the trip was silent, and John leaned his arm against the window, his eyes watching the street. He figured he'd tell his mother about his engagement if she was home, eat something quick, and then head upstairs to call Michael. He would leave the unpacking for tomorrow—or the next day, depending on his mood towards the suitcase—and run over to Sarah's to spend some time with her.

Soon the car pulled up to his apartment building and John got out, paid the driver his fee, and pulled his heavy suitcase out of the trunk. He was sure his keys was somewhere in his bag, but John didn't want to go through it, so he headed upstairs and knocked on the apartment door, hoping his mother would answer.

Thankfully, his mother was indeed home and she welcomed him inside with a hug and a kiss on the cheek. John laughed and pushed his luggage aside as he closed the door.

"How did you cope without me?" he asked her in a teasing manner.

"I'm fine. Plenty of things to do while you're gone," she said brightly, not taking the bait. "But now I'm glad to see my son. How was the trip? Did you take lots of pictures?"

"Too many, and the trip was great," replied John. He smiled a little too widely and his mother looked at him expectedly.

"What happened, John?" she asked, folding her arms across her chest. "Did something exciting take place?"

"Well ..." began John, and he launched straight into his engagement. His mother, as expected, was thrilled over the news, and she didn't stop talking about it until John retired to his room that night. He perhaps should have waited until tomorrow to tell her, as he was tired and needed sleep—not to mention he had a lot of work to do.

A few calls were made to Michael, asking about work and what projects were currently underway. John scratched some notes down on paper, scheduling a few dates and important things to remember, and then he called Sarah, wanting to hear her voice before he went to sleep that night. She was incredibly sleepy, her usual bright voice soft and weary. He didn't keep her long on the phone and hung up after a few minutes, letting her get to bed. He went to sleep shortly after, feeling the tug on his eyelids, beckoning him to dreamland.

The following day, John headed over to Sarah's house, now wanting to escape from work and just be with his fiancé for a little while before work became too demanding. He was lying on her bed with her, and watched as she turned off the DVD player and tossed the remote onto the desk beside the bed. They had been watching a movie, though John couldn't for the life of him remember what it was about or how it had even ended. He had been too distracted by Sarah, wanting to touch and kiss her. Now that the movie was over, he planned to do the things he had been itching to do since yesterday.

He reached out and touched her hand, but Sarah

smiled slyly and hid it behind her back. He then slid his hand along her leg up to her hip and tightened his arms around her, wanting to become as close as possible.

"John!" Sarah struggled in his grip, a little breathless. "You're actually hurting me."

He loosened his hold a little. "I love you so much."

"So you say," said Sarah with a scowl. "But lovers don't smother each other!"

John laughed and leaned in towards her. He kissed her tenderly on the lips, but she slipped out of his grasp and snatched up a pillow, hitting him over the head with it.

"Hey!" cried John, flinging up his hands in defence. "What was that for?"

Sarah simply laughed. The stuffing was coming out of the pillow at one corner and she pulled off the casing and grabbed a handful of cotton. "*That* was for squeezing my ribs apart. Now stand up with me and celebrate."

Celebrate? John stared up at her while she stood, unbalanced, on the bed, and she took her handful of cotton and threw it into the air like confetti. The fan on the desk was blowing and the wind took the pieces of fabric, sending them whirling around the room. *Well, all right, then*, thought John, feeling equally silly at this moment. He also stood up and took the pillow from Sarah, ripping it down the side. They both took a giant fistful of cotton and tossed it upwards, allowing it to fall around them as they stumbled around on top of the bed.

Sarah laughed as John tripped and fell back down, but he quickly pulled her along with him, landing amongst the pieces of cotton and ripped pillow fragments. He gazed long and hard into her eyes, seeing the energy and happiness contained within, and waited for her to do something.

She leaned across him, pressing herself tight against him, and kissed his cheek, then his forehead, and eyelids before moving her lips down upon his neck. John gently rolled her over and leaned into her, allowing his lips to push onto hers. The noise of the fan died as John deepened his kisses. He felt Sarah's cool hands under his shirt, running up his back, and he pulled the cloth from his skin, tossing the garment to the floor. He leaned back against her, and drove all thoughts from his mind.

John had brought his bike over to Sarah's house that day, wanting to take a ride out to the Hudson River. Sarah agreed to join him, so they strapped on some helmets and headed out, feeling the gentle spring breeze grace their skin as they peddled through the city. It was

the perfect day for riding, and John was glad they had managed to get out of the house before the day was completely over. Despite how much he enjoyed intimate moments with Sarah, he enjoyed moments like these just as much, and he couldn't wait to peddle over the Brooklyn Bridge with her for the first time this year.

She was animated as usual when they reached the river, stopping to look over the side from time to time. John eventually told her to stay on her bike and enjoy the ride; they would come back another time to admire the sights. Though, when she stuck to the plan, she would speed ahead and cross in front of him, teasing. John simply smiled and attempted to do the same, though she was a little sneaky and often avoided the trick.

After a while they left the bridge and found a restaurant. The ride was tiring and they needed to eat up and take a short break before heading back home.

It was in that moment—while sitting at an outside table munching down some cheesy nachos— that John suddenly realized that Sarah's birthday was in a few days. With all the commotion lately, he had completely forgotten about it, but now he had to think of something to get her. Maybe something useful for her job would be best, as he had already given her a few pieces of nice jewelry.

I'll have to think on it, John said to himself, and he paid the bill and hopped back on his bike.

CHAPTER 13

It was her birthday again, which meant another year had passed. Sarah took a deep breath and looked around the living room of her home. Amanda had decorated the place nicely, with balloons and streamers and flowers hanging off every piece of furniture and plastered upon the walls. Her cousin had spent the morning decorating and plotting while Sarah had been out. It was a small gathering, with only a few close friends and relatives attending. Some had come in from out of town, while others were co-workers. They had bought her a cake in the shape of a courthouse, which Sarah had laughed at, and it was now sitting on the table, candles all lit, awaiting the birthday girl to blow them out.

"Make a wish!" called Amanda, standing nearby with a camera poised. She winked.

Sarah flushed and tried to ignore her cousin and her embarrassing ways. She was about to blow out the candles when she spotted William under the archway of the living room, just arriving to the party. She beckoned him over, saving herself momentarily from the attention she was about to receive.

"Happy birthday, Sarah!" he greeted. He handed her a bouquet of purple and blue flowers. "May God bless you, and I hope your day turns into the best day of the year."

Sarah hugged him and accepted the flowers, smiling brightly. "Thank you, Bill! They're beautiful! And I hope you're right about the best day wish."

"Hey, dude!" John meandered over towards them, a glass of wine in his hand.

"Oh, John." William nodded in greeting. "What's up?"

"Just enjoying the party." John motioned for Michael to come over. "I want you to meet a friend of mine."

Sarah moved away from them and back to the cake, where Amanda was anxiously awaiting her cousin to cut it so she could take more pictures. Sarah gave her an exasperated look but Amanda ignored it and grinned before raising the camera to eye-level. She was dedicated to having as many pictures of this day as possible.

What can I wish for? Sarah thought. She already had everything she could ever want: great job, great boyfriend, great friends. Her life was going pretty good lately—no, it was going more than good. It was perfect, and she wouldn't change a thing.

Sarah pursed her lips together and finally blew

out the candles, deciding just to wish for everyone's happiness, as she really couldn't think of anything else. Amanda clicked down on the camera, a bright flash filling the room. The clapping and cheering began, and then came the singing. Sarah blushed even more at that, and started cutting pieces off the cake, giving one to each of her friends. John took the knife from her after she was done and cut a piece off for her. Sarah found a fork and dug in, delighted that Amanda had ordered her favorite kind of cake.

After the cake, Sarah did her rounds around the room. Everyone seemed to want to talk with her, and she caught up with a few old friends and family members. There was no mention of work at the party, which relieved her. That was the last thing she wanted to think about today.

They played a few party games. Michael and Amanda seemed to be fairly good at pretty much everything, and Sarah found herself cheering them on most of the time. There was music also and second helpings of the cake. Sarah licked the icing off her fingers as she swallowed the last piece on her plate and was about to go for some more food when Amanda pulled her away from the table. She protested wildly as she was dragged to the center of the room, and her stomach rolled over when she saw the devious look in her cousin's eyes.

Oh boy, thought Sarah. *What now?*

✳ ✳ ✳

A woman cleared her throat and William turned his attention from the wine glass in his hand to Amanda, Sarah's cousin. She was standing at the center of the room now with a bright smile upon her face, and William was curious to know what she was about to announce, for surely—judging by the look on her face—there was something important to share with everyone.

"Attention everyone!" called Amanda, tapping a fork against her glass to further draw eyes towards her. "Tonight I have some good news. You all know my dear cousin Sarah, of course, and John, her beloved, who she has been dating for quite some time now." She lifted her glass to them, and Sarah smiled shyly, slipping her hand into John's. William grudgingly looked away from them and back to Amanda. "During their trip to India, John decided to propose to my dear cousin. They'll be tying the knot soon!"

There was more clapping and a few people whistled, causing Sarah's blush to increase. She hid her face in John's shoulder and he laughed.

William simply clutched onto his glass and stared at the couple, his throat dry. That was it, then. Sarah would be married and his last remaining chance to have her was over. It sucked. It more than sucked.

He hated the feeling that washed over him. He hated looking at them, happy and in love. *He* wanted to be the one she loved, but that would never happen, especially not after this.

Downing his last drop of wine, William placed the glass on the table filled with food and empty plates and made his way over to the couple, knowing that he had to say something or Sarah would be upset about it. He didn't want to go near them right now, but he had to, if only for Sarah's happiness. Luckily, she was alone. John was busy chatting to Michael, who he had just been introduced to.

"Congratulations, Sarah!" he forced out, hoping his smile looked genuine. "You're finally getting married. I didn't know you were ready for it."

Sarah laughed and ducked her head, still embarrassed. "Yeah, I have been since I met John," she admitted, which William didn't like in the least. "There was just this feeling I had, you know? You just realize 'hey, he's the one!'." She placed her hand behind her neck and looked sheepishly up at William. "I'm sure someday you'll find your true love, too, Bill. You're such a nice guy—you may even beat me to the altar!"

William gave a forced smile as she laughed. "Thanks, Sarah," he said gently. He wouldn't be at the altar for a long time. Getting over Sarah would take some time, and it was something he knew he absolutely had to do if he wanted to move forward with life. But right now he didn't want to do that. He just couldn't let go yet.

"Excuse me, guys," said John, cutting in. He glanced to Sarah and held out his hand. "Would you like to dance, my dear?"

Sarah smiled at him and then looked to William. "No, John. I'm not ready to dance quite yet."

"Oh, come on!" pleaded John. He gave her an insistent look. "I know how well you dance. Please? *Please*. Pretty please?"

Sarah finally caved in and laughed, shaking her head. "Oh, all right," she said, taking his hand. "If you're going to be like that, I'll dance with you." She stole a quick glance at William. "I'll talk to you later?"

"Later," agreed William, sulkily watching them waltz off.

He headed back to the table and poured himself another glass of wine, while at the center of the room other couples were now joining the birthday girl and her beloved to dance around them. William studied them, his eyes sullen, as he sipped back his drink—perhaps a little too quickly. He wished there was something stronger here, as he couldn't take the loving way Sarah looked at that man. There was nothing wrong with him. He had a good job; he was decent; he made her happy. William just hated him because he had chosen the one woman who William loved. He had stolen her away.

Why couldn't I be the one in this picture, dancing with you? he thought grimly. He took another gulp of his wine and began imagining himself out there on the dance floor with her, the look in her eyes now reflecting back at him. What he wouldn't give for her to look at him like that, to see him as he saw her. He could hold her like John did, and dance just as well. He saw them dancing together now, his arm looped around her waist, his hand slipped into hers, and she was smiling like she never had before.

"Bill?"

William turned to his right and saw her standing there, beautiful in the dim atmosphere of the room. She lifted her delicate hand and touched his face, a soft smile upon her ruby lips.

"Won't you dance with me, Bill?" she asked tenderly, tilting her head a little to the side. Her auburn hair fell around her pale shoulders.

"I ... I can't," said William quietly, reaching up to touch her hand. It was soft, and warm like sunshine.

But she was gone in an instant, and he looked back to the center of the room to see Sarah out there with John still, laughing and having the time of her life. William placed his glass of unfinished wine on the table, his hand slightly shaking. He rubbed his eyes tiredly. He had conjured her up, it seemed, which meant he was a little too drunk on both alcohol and emotions.

I should go home, he thought bitterly. *If I stay any longer, I may end up saying something I shouldn't.*

Without giving the newly engaged couple another glance, William grabbed his coat on the couch and left, not saying a word to anyone.

❊ ❊ ❊

"I have a surprise for you!" said John, grinning broadly as he walked backwards out the front door. Sarah followed him, not quite sure what he was talking about. He had already given her tickets to see one of her favorite plays at the local theater and she liked that gift well enough, so what was he about to show her now?

She stopped, stunned, when she saw it: a Mercedes Benz parked in her driveway. Was *that* what John had driven up in earlier? She hadn't been at the door to greet him and she hadn't looked outside since he arrived. She remembered discussing the idea of buying a car a few weeks ago with him, but she had no idea *this* was the car he had in mind and she didn't know he had bought it or was planning to buy it soon.

"Wow," she breathed, a little breathless. "It's a nice looking car."

"I agree," said John elatedly. "I love this model. So ..." He looked excitedly towards her. "How about we take it for a spin?"

"Oh, I don't know ..." murmured Sarah, as she

glanced back to the house. She hadn't told anyone she had come out here. "I mean, I have the party inside and—"

"We won't be long." John hopped back up the steps where Sarah was standing. He took both her hands and kissed her. "Please, Sarah? Please ... *please* ..."

Sarah sighed and rolled her eyes. He was doing that thing again, and she found it hard to say no to him when he begged like that. She gave him a wide smile and gave in once more tonight. "Fine! One quick drive and then we have to get back to the party."

"Deal!" John opened the passenger side door for her and she got inside, already impressed with the modern interior. John hurried around to the other side and jumped into the driver's seat with ease. He started up the engine, which roared to life almost instantly, and shifted the gear into drive. Sarah barely had time to fasten her seatbelt before they were cruising down the street.

They were out onto the highway in no time at all, the power of the vehicle making it easy to pass other cars and maneuver nicely through the city. Sarah had been relaxed for a while, but now she was slightly on edge as they drove along the near-empty highway.

"This car is fantastic," said John animatedly. He pressed a button on the dash and the radio came to life, filling the car with soft music. "I'm enjoying the speed nicely."

Sarah gripped her hand onto the edge of her seat and gave John a wary look. "That's nice, but I'm a little scared. Just be careful, all right?"

"Oh, Sarah ..." said John, shaking his head. "Rest assured. I'm a fantastic driver."

"Okay," murmured Sarah, though still uneasy.

There wasn't much traffic on the highway, but that was what worried Sarah most. John was still speeding up and it was completely unnecessary. She was about to tell him that they should probably be heading back to the party now, as the guests would be wondering where they ran off to, when John began speeding up to pass a couple of cars in front of them.

"Oh my God, John!" Sarah pressed her hand against the dashboard and her heart flipped over in her chest. They were going way too fast! "Slow down before you kill us!"

"Relax!" John called back, still chuckling at her fear.

The Mercedes glided easily past the two cars and John flicked over his blinker, ready to move back into the other lane. Sarah eased back into her seat.

To their left, the sound of angry horns blasted through the air, and Sarah's heart finally dropped to the bottom of her stomach. She glanced past John and through the window to see a transport truck closing in on them, its bulky frame a terrifying shadow in the night. John loudly swore and hastily swerved to the right. Unused to the feel of the car, he pulled in too fast and the car spun completely around in a circle, tires screeching. Sarah screamed and grabbed onto her seatbelt as the cars in the lane propelled towards them, horns honking and lights blinding their vision.

Everything afterwards was a blur. There was the sound of cracking metal, shrieking tires, steel cascading down the highway, and Sarah's own breathing as she struggled to hang onto consciousness. Dark shapes swirled before her, fading in and out of her gaze, and she saw John out on the street, unmoving and covered in blood.

Her hand wanted to reach out towards him, but she realized she couldn't move her hand, or anything else, and she felt liquid pour down across her forehead and into her eyes, further blinding her. She grasped that it was her own blood that she felt and she whimpered into the night, feeling utterly helpless.

Darkness finally overtook her, and all sound vanished.

CHAPTER 14

Something bright lingered overhead. Every time Sarah tried to open her eyes, the blinding light forced her lids to close again. There was pain also. It ran up and down her legs and through her fingers towards her palms. An unbearable throbbing pulsated at her temples and when she finally managed to open her eyes, the room spun uncontrollably. She grasped something to her left and held onto whatever it was. Slowly she pulled herself up and looked around.

White walls, the smell of antiseptics, a cool draft from above. She was in a hospital.

A shot of pain in her legs caused Sarah to cringe and curl her knees towards her stomach. She gripped the bed sheets and let out a few jagged breaths.

Why was she here? She couldn't remember. There was a party and cake …

Yes, her birthday was yesterday. She knew that much. Her head was pounding and when she touched it, there were bandages wrapped around her temple.

Did something happen at the party? Sarah thought.

She couldn't think of anything going wrong. She didn't recall a fire or some other dangerous accident occurring.

Bandages were also around her hands and—when she lifted the sheets—her legs. There were bruises in other places and little scratches. Sarah was mystified. She took a deep breath to calm herself and closed her eyes. It was time to think back to last night.

Amanda had decorated the house for her birthday. She came home afterwards and people started to arrive for the party. John gave her tickets to a play; William brought flowers; Amanda took her picture as she cut the cake. There was dancing and ...

Sarah's eyes flashed open. She had left the house with John. He wanted to show her something.

There was an icy tingle running up her arms and along her neck now. The pieces were starting to come together. She was starting to remember what had happened that night.

The car, thought Sarah, a wave of dizziness taking her. The car. The highway. The screeching horns and blinding lights.

And John ... lying on the road out of reach.

"John," whispered Sarah, hands shaking. "John ... JOHN!"

Someone entered the room then, hearing Sarah shout, and made their way over to the bed. Sarah was vaguely aware of their presence, not even knowing if they were male or female, before she leapt from the bed—ignoring the pain in her legs—and pushed past the person. Another came into the room and Sarah saw her path blocked.

No, no! I must get to John! she desperately thought.

A sharp prick was felt at the back of her neck and Sarah stopped, feeling dizzy all of a sudden. Hands led her back to the bed and she lay down, tired. She closed her eyes and slept.

❉ ❉ ❉

Hours passed before Sarah was awake again, though a nurse was sitting in a chair by the bedside, watching her this time. Sarah sat up, feeling groggy.

"John ... where is John?" she struggled to ask.

"The man who was in the car with you is now in our intensive care unit," explained the nurse. Her light hair was tied up into a knot. "His mother was here a short while ago and then left to go back to her son's room, so there's no need to worry."

"Please," begged Sarah, tossing back the sheets. There was no point in reassuring her; she was already worried. "Please take me to him."

The nurse crossed her arms and frowned in disapproval. "You're in no condition to leave this room, and don't try it again."

Sarah began to sob. "Please, I beg you. I *have* to see him. I'll come back afterwards. I just need to see that he's all right. Can you bring me to him?"

The nurse wasn't happy but she left the room and returned with a wheelchair. Sarah stumbled into it, her legs still weak, and anxiously glanced from side to side as the nurse wheeled her down the hospital hall, checking each room to see if John was inside.

The accident rushed back into Sarah's thoughts once more and she shook her head, feeling sick. John was going to be all right. He was strong—a fighter. He would pull through this. An image of him lying on the road, bloody and unconscious roared within her mind and Sarah felt hot pricks at the corner of her eyes.

"Here we are," said the nurse, stopping the wheelchair.

Sarah used the ledge of the window in front of her to pull herself up. She leaned against it and peered inside. The room was frightening, a mess of machines and dark corners. John was lying on a bed at the center of it all, a mask supplying air to his lungs over his face and cords running from his arms and head. He was on life support and a machine next to the bed displayed a slow heart rate.

Sarah struggled to breath for a moment. Her legs gave out and she fell back into the wheelchair. John was ... he was ...

"NO!" Sarah cried and placed a hand upon the arm of the wheelchair for support. John was going to be fine! She had already decided that before now, and he was strong—he would make it out of here with her!

"Sarah?" The owner of the name glanced up to see Jessica walking slowly towards her. She seemed to have been speaking with a doctor a few seconds before, as the surgeon turned abruptly on his heel and headed down the hall, no doubt rushing off to see another patient.

"Jessica," whispered Sarah, feeling comfort in knowing another who loved John was nearby.

Jessica touched Sarah's shoulder and squeezed it. There were tears in her eyes and her skin underneath was red. "How are you feeling, Sarah?" she asked. Sarah simply nodded, too upset to speak. "You were unconscious when I was in your room earlier. I'm glad you're all right now." She took out a tissue from her pocket and wiped the corners of her eyes. "John's condition is critical. He's been unconscious most of the night, and now ..." She gave a soft sob. "Now he's in a coma."

"No ..." Sarah's lower lip trembled. She gazed down at her lap and squeezed her eyes shut. It was all a horrible nightmare. She would wake up from this and go back to her happy, perfect life.

John was fine. He was going to be fine.

No sooner had the bus pulled to a stop when William jumped out through the sliding door. He hurried through the Mount Sinai hospital's crowded parking lot and entered through the front doors, heading through the waiting area and towards the receptionist. She was busy taking a call when William approached, and so he waited impatiently, shifting from one foot to the other, until she had finished.

"Sorry for the wait," she said, as she slid her chair towards the window. "How can I help you, sir?"

"I'm looking for Sarah Jane Miller," explained William in a rush. "She was in a car accident and brought here last night."

"Okay, please wait a few moments," said the receptionist. She started typing on her computer keyboard, and William waited fretfully as she searched. "Yes, Sarah Miller is currently in the emergency ward."

She told William the number of the room and which way he should go and he left the reception area. His nerves were all in knots as he made his way towards Sarah's room. He felt so angry, partially towards John for placing Sarah in such danger and partially towards himself for leaving the party last night. He kept thinking that maybe if he had stayed, if Sarah had come back to talk with him, she wouldn't have gone out for a drive, or if she had gone for a drive it would have been different because the time had been changed.

But she had gone out in that car and she had been seriously hurt. William curled his fingers towards his palm and formed a fist. If John was okay, he would give him something to hurt about.

William's head was still pounding from his hangover, but his senses were thankfully clear enough to navigate to Sarah's room. He took a deep breath before going inside, fearing for the worst. He let it out when he saw her sitting up in bed. She looked to be physically all right despite the few bandages that were on her wrists and head.

"Sarah." Her eyes momentarily lit up when she saw him, but the light quickly vanished and was replaced with a mix of fear and sadness. He moved to her bedside. "Are you okay?"

"Yeah." Sarah gave a slow nod. "But John ... John is in a coma. He's bad, William. He's—"

"Sarah, Sarah ..." William gripped her arm firmly and waited for her to calm down a little. Her breathing was irregular and tears were streaming down her face. She wiped them off one by one, drying her hands on the bed sheets. She was a mess and it made his heart hurt to see her this way. "You're a brave girl, Sarah. Don't cry. Stay strong. You'll get through this."

She nodded again, a little more firmly this time, and her eyes moved to the doorway. William looked over his shoulder to see an older woman come into the room, a tissue in her hand. He instantly knew that this was John's mother.

"Bill, this is Jessica," introduced Sarah, her lip trembling. "Jessica is John's mother."

William exchanged both greetings and condolences with her. He wasn't sure what to say to this woman. Moments ago he had wanted to punch John for causing Sarah pain, but now he simply pitied the man.

For Sarah's sake, he hoped John made it through this.

❈ ❈ ❈

Sarah was back at John's lonely window, peering in through the glass. He wasn't doing any better. The machine next to the bed that measured his heart rate was erratic, the waves on screen going up and down. Sarah could barely stand it. John was still on life support and the doctors hadn't given them any good news about his condition. His chest moved faintly up and down, though that seemed to be the only indication that he was still alive.

Sarah could stand without the wheelchair now. She had been discharged this morning after another thorough inspection, but she lingered still, hoping that John would come around and be able to leave with her—or at least open his eyes and look at his fiancé.

But his face was slack and still covered by that horrid mask.

Sarah hugged her arms around her middle and hung her head, feeling on onslaught of tears rushing forward again. She was tired of crying but she could do nothing else. Everything had been so perfect lately, and now it was all crashing around her feet. Her world was threatening to fall apart.

"Sarah, are you okay?" William approached her side, a worried look upon his face. She studied him for a moment through her watery eyes, wondering why he just didn't go home. He stayed the night at the hospital with her and Jessica, though he didn't have to. She knew he was just being a good friend, but he didn't need to put himself through this. She was doing okay—well enough to leave, at least.

"Sorry, Bill," said Sarah, drifting away from her thoughts. She wiped her sleeve across her face, mopping up the tears, but they came again, flooding her cheeks. "I just ... I can't bear to see him like this. I can't think about ... I don't *want* to think about ..."

"Sarah ..." William reached out his hand and she took it, allowing herself to be pulled into a comforting hug. "I know this is difficult, but you have to be strong," he whispered. "You have more struggles to come, so keep your tears in and prepare yourself to fight against the odds. You'll need to find all the possible ways to save his life when the time comes."

Sarah nodded against his shoulder and pulled away when she saw Jessica approach.

"Sarah, please don't cry anymore," said the older woman, trying hard to smile. "John is very lucky to have someone like you beside him, someone who loves him so much." She gazed up at the large clock over their heads on the wall and turned back to Sarah. "You should go home and get some rest. The doctor released you hours ago."

"I'll drop her off," offered William.

"No!" Sarah gently grabbed Jessica's hands, a pleading look in her eyes. "Please, I want to stay here with you and watch over John."

Jessica leaned forward and kissed Sarah lightly on the forehead. "No, my child. You've had a trying ordeal. You need to get out of this place and rest in your own bed—you need to recover. Don't worry about John. I'll be here. He will be fine." She squeezed Sarah's hands. "Keep yourself strong. I'll call you if anything changes."

Sarah slowly nodded. She was tired, and the hospital atmosphere wasn't helping. Jessica was probably right. She needed to get out of here. "Okay. I'll be back in the morning, though."

"Then I'll see you tomorrow morning," said Jessica, letting go of Sarah's hands. "When you come in tomorrow I'll go home and rest while you watch over him." She turned to William, a sad smile upon her face. "Thank you for everything, dear."

"Don't mention it. Anything to help," replied William.

"Sarah, William is a nice guy," said Jessica, and she looked back to the window where her son lay just beyond the glass. "You're lucky to have such a wonderful friend in your life. He helped and supported me a lot today."

Sarah glanced to William, a little surprised, but the tired look in her friend's eyes revealed more than he said. "I know," she said quietly, smiling softly.

"Thanks," murmured William sheepishly.

"Good night, my babe," said Jessica, giving Sarah another kiss on the forehead. "Take care of yourself. You can't welcome John back if you aren't feeling well."

"You're right." Sarah gave her a quick hug, a little faith restored within her. "Good night."

Sarah followed William out of the intensive care unit and towards the exit. There was a sudden longing when she stepped through the emergency wing's doors and out

into the fresh air, as though moving away from the hospital shook her very soul. She didn't want to leave John there in that room, hooked up to all those machines and wires, but Jessica was right. She needed to get home and have a good night's sleep, to recover her strength and rekindle her hope.

She wondered if sleep was even possible.

CHAPTER 15

The sky had been clear when they had left the hospital, but now the atmosphere overhead was becoming quite grey. A few drops of rain leaked from the heavens and more followed. Soon, William and Sarah found themselves running down the sidewalk towards a small coffee shop, their heels clicking off the ground. The rain had soaked through their clothes somewhat as they moved into the shelter of the store, and William shook the drops off his shoulders.

They sat at an outdoor table under a long roof, feeling both uncomfortable and anxious. William noticed that Sarah was tense, her eyes drifting from himself to the street they had just gone down. He knew she was worried about John, but there was nothing she could do for him.

"Don't worry, Sarah," said William comfortingly. "John will be fine. He'll come around soon."

Sarah smiled and nodded, relaxing her shoulders. She seemed to be trying to fall back into her normal habits, but her eyes betrayed her. The light and happiness that rested within her pupils was no longer there. There was no energy to her smile or no life to her being.

"Would you like anything?" offered William, motioning to the shop.

"No, thanks," replied Sarah, again trying to smile. It wasn't fooling anyone.

"I think it might do you some good," said William, waving over a waiter. "It might take some stress off your shoulders, relax you a little."

Sarah watched as the server approached them and she slowly nodded. "Okay. That sounds good."

William wanted to tell her that he was here for her, no matter what, that he would stay by her side, but he felt a confession like that just wouldn't do at the moment. At the very least he could take care of her until she got home safely. But still …

Sarah was biting her lower lip, gently tugging at her rosy flesh with her teeth. William wanted so desperately to kiss her, then, to lean across the table and feel those lips against his own. Heat ran up and down his body and he curled his hand into a fist under the table, reminding himself to keep under control. Sarah wasn't his. She was John's fiancé, and therefore would never be his. And John was in the hospital. The realization of his feelings and thoughts caused William to shake his head in shame.

"What is it?" asked Sarah, curious of his action.

"Nothing ..." murmured William, feeling even guiltier now. "I was ... I was just thinking of how afraid I was when I heard you were in the hospital. Thank God. He saved your life, and He'll save John's life, too."

Sarah sipped her coffee and placed it slowly down on the table, her fingers warming on the cup. "Thank you for everything, William. It's been a rough few days."

William simply smiled. "There's no need to thank me. You know what they say: a friend in need is a friend indeed."

"Yeah, I know." Sarah offered the tiniest of smiles and was silent for a few moments, as if thinking upon something. "You are a true friend," she finally said, and glanced out towards the road again. "The rain has stopped. We should get going before it decides to start up again."

"Okay," said William.

He paid for the coffee and left a small tip before returning to the street and their walk home. Sarah's house was still a long ways off, and William wasn't sure why she didn't want to take the bus right now. It would have been faster, but she insisted upon walking for some reason. Perhaps focusing on taking one step after another filled her thoughts, while sitting on a bus would only force her to think upon John and his condition.

William gazed up at the grim sky in contemplation. If things became worse, Sarah would need him more than ever, but he was afraid of her needing him. The way he felt about her ... surely she would find out if he spent that much time with her, and then she would become angry and shun him. He didn't want that.

A few drops of rain bounced off William's head and he sighed in annoyance. Sarah said nothing. Her eyes were on the ground, distant and sad.

"Sarah," said William slowly, suddenly realizing that they were close to his house, "do you want to stay at my place tonight? It's just down the street. I don't think the rain is going to stop, and I don't want you getting sick and winding up in the hospital again."

Sarah nodded and started towards William's street. "Okay. Thank you, Bill."

The slight shower turned into a heavy downpour, and they were running again. William drew his key out of his pocket as he ran and leapt up two steps at a time to his door. He unlocked it and ushered Sarah inside and out of the rain. He flicked on the light and pried off his boots—they were soaking wet and would no doubt take hours to dry.

"I'll get you a towel," he said to Sarah, before moving into the bathroom. He found a long one and

returned to Sarah, allowing her to dry off her hair and face with it.

"Your dress is soaking," commented William, frowning as Sarah's clothes stuck to her skin. She sneezed and handed the towel back to William. "Hold on. I'll get you something to wear."

He found a small shirt in the back of his closet and a pair of pajamas that didn't quite fit. Both things would be too big on her, but she couldn't be picky at the moment. William gave her the clothes and she drifted off into the living room to change.

He left the hall and retrieved a shirt for himself in his wardrobe, feeling the one he wore clinging to his skin. He moved from the bedroom back into the hall, pulling off his wet shirt, when he saw that the living room door was slightly ajar.

Through the slim crack, William could see Sarah. She was standing in the moonlight of the night, her skin gleaming in the pale light. Her dress was on the floor and she stood there in her bra and underwear, her hair cascading down her fair back. William studied her legs, her hips, the curve from there to her bra, and her hair as it shifted around her exposed skin.

He wanted to go in there and hold her against his own bare chest, to kiss her uncovered flesh and make her his. The thought drove him mad, and he diverted his gaze, feeling the heat rush up and down his body. He rushed into the bathroom and threw on his shirt, not wanting to stand out in the hall—half out of fear that she may look towards him and half out of fear that he may *want* her to look at him. Nothing good would come from that. She wouldn't find him desirable, not with John on her mind.

She hadn't been fired from her job or failed a case; her fiancé was in the hospital in critical condition. The only thing that could make her feel better now was his swift recovery.

William hung his wet shirt on the shower rod and moved out towards the drawing room. Sarah was already there, wearing his clothes. He paused for a moment, studying her. She looked gorgeous in his bedclothes, and his desire roared to life again, threatening to undo him.

Shut up, he told himself. *She isn't yours, so keep your mouth shut.*

"What would you like for dinner?" he asked, smiling a little.

"Anything is good," said Sarah quietly, picking a loose strand of fabric at the base of the shirt.

"Okay." William frowned at the sadness in her eyes. "I'll make something quick so you can get some sleep, okay?"

"No." Sarah looked up from the shirt. "I'll help you. Just tell me what you want to make."

"Okay, let's get to work, then."

They headed into the kitchen, and William remembered the last time Sarah had been here. It was a long while ago now, and John had come, as well. William remembered how surprised he was when Sarah had shown up on his door, and how disappointed he became when John also appeared.

Stop it, he reminded himself. *Stop being jealous. She isn't yours!*

He pulled some ingredients out of the fridge and cupboards and got started on some pasta. It was quick and easy, and his homemade sauce would at least satisfy Sarah's appetite.

She assisted him, cutting up peppers and mushrooms to go in the sauce. William chatted with her as he worked, and she kept the conversation going. He felt happy for a moment, enjoying his time in the kitchen with her. He could picture them doing this often, being together like this as a couple, but the image was ruined when he looked back to Sarah. There was a tear rolling down her cheek. It slid from her chin down to the counter.

She was miserable, and William suddenly felt the same way. Every time he saw her like this he just wanted to cry along with her. Why couldn't she be happy? Why was the world throwing such sadness her way? She didn't deserve any of this pain, and he wished he could take it away, but he knew the only person who could do that was John.

That—also—made William miserable.

✳ ✳ ✳

Even in William's king-sized bed Sarah felt uncomfortable and lost. She felt alone, even though William was just a few rooms over. She had never felt this way before—this sense of sorrow and loneliness. It was keeping her up, this feeling, and she wanted it to desperately go away. She needed her strength for tomorrow. *John* needed her strength. She had to stay happy for him. She had to keep hope and know that he would get better.

Still, as much as she told herself that he would be fine and everything would work out, sleep didn't come. Her eyes shut and she let her mind fall silent, but dreamland stayed just out of reach. She knew it was pointless to stay in bed and do nothing, as sleep would never come that way, so she slid back the covers and

touched her feet to the floor. William was sleeping in the drawing room. She headed that way, hoping that perhaps being near him would cause her loneliness to dissipate.

William was sleeping on the couch, a single blanket pulled across himself. It was slipping to the floor and Sarah bent and drew it back over her friend, making sure the cold didn't get to him. She then turned towards the window and stretched open the curtains, allowing the moonlight to embrace her.

The night sky was dark, though the stars were all out, keeping the full moon company. Sarah sat on the chair under the window and leaned against the glass, keeping her eyes locked with the sky. The clouds were slowly enveloping the moon, surrounding it in a pale cover. It was mesmerizing, and Sarah watched on and on, becoming lost in the night's beauty.

Soon, darkness became light, and dawn stretched up over the edge of the horizon. The sky turned red and orange and Sarah watched on, her eyes dark and tired now. The reality of her life had sunk in over the course of the night, and she knew she had to grow stronger. She had to face whatever awaited her in the following days. John could get better, but he could get worse, and she had to be ready for that. She didn't know exactly how to prepare for such a thing, and she certainly didn't want to think about it or believe that such a thing could happen, but she could start with smiling and having faith in herself.

A slight noise behind her caused Sarah to turn around. William was waking up, and when he saw her he stared for a moment, a little dazed and perhaps confused as to why she was sitting in the drawing room.

"Sarah ... what's wrong?" he rubbed his eyes and propped himself up on his elbow. "Didn't you sleep at all?"

Sarah saw the worried look on his face and stood up from the chair. He had been so concerned about her state of mind yesterday, but now she had to reassure him that she was fine and was strong enough to hold herself up. She didn't need him worrying about her like that, and she would make sure that Jessica didn't worry either.

Sarah flashed him a wide smile, and he stared in surprise at her.

"Good morning, William," she said brightly. "I tried to sleep but I couldn't, so I came out here. I hope I didn't wake you."

William was still staring. "Sarah … no, you didn't, but—"

"William, I want to go out now," interrupted Sarah, not wanting to know where he was going with his line of thinking. She didn't want anyone asking if she was okay anymore. "I think I'll drop by the nearest church on my way to the hospital and say a few prayers for John's recovery."

There was a small sigh on William's lips. "Okay," he said softly. "I think that's a good idea."

"I'll be back in a few minutes." Sarah left the drawing room and checked the laundry area for her dress. She fetched it out of the dryer and headed into the bathroom to change out of William's clothes. Her hair was tangled but she found a brush and straightened it out nicely. Her makeup had been smudged in the rain and she wiped it off with some tissue. She splashed water on her face, dried herself off, and folded William's clothes up before leaving the bathroom.

Sarah placed the clothes on William's bed and returned to the drawing room. William was sitting up on the couch now, rubbing the palms of his hands against his face. Sarah cleared her throat and put on a smile before he removed his hands and looked up.

"I'm ready to go," she said. She fetched her purse where it was sitting on the table. "So, have a good day."

"Hang on." William stood up and tossed the blanket back on the couch. "I think I'll meet you at the hospital when you're done at the church."

Sarah smiled and hoisted her purse up onto her shoulder. "Okay. I'll look for you there."

"Best of luck today, Sarah." William gave her a considerate look. "Don't push yourself too hard."

"I won't," she promised.

She then waved and left the house, heading down the porch steps to the street. It was a beautiful morning, and she had a feeling that things would be better today. As long as she had hope and faith on her side, John would recover and her life would go back to its perfect ways again.

CHAPTER 16

A soft light filled the old church. Color flowed in through the stain glass windows, creating spots of red, blue, yellow, and green on the floor. It was empty today, and even the priest was nowhere to be found. Still, it was a charming and majestic building, with a high ceiling and ancient archways. Pictures were depicted on the walls of scenes from the Bible, and the carved figure of Jesus Christ upon a cross sat at the back of the church, a crown of thorns upon His head.

Sarah was kneeling just before the statue, her eyes clenched shut and her hands folded together. The silence of the church allowed her to think out what she wanted to say, and although it sounded like selfish wishes to make, she couldn't think of any other way to put it. She wanted John to live. She desired his good health to return. It was not often that she prayed, and perhaps that was why it sounded so selfish to her.

"Jesus, lord in heaven, please save my love," she prayed aloud. "Please rescue him from this battle he is fighting. I can't live my life without him—he means everything to me! Please forgive us, forgive our sins and wrongdoings. I know you are kind, so show me that kindness. I pray, give us your blessing."

Sarah paused, wondering if she had said enough, if her prayers would be answered in their current form. She wasn't an expert in praying, but she was told throughout her childhood that prayers were always heard, no matter how small or large they were, or how short or long.

Feeling confident that she had done it right, Sarah blew out the candle in front of her and left the church.

✳ ✳ ✳

The hospital would always be a busy place, and Sarah found herself weaving through the main lobby past the crowd and wandered into a hallway that led to the intensive care unit. She felt at ease walking down this corridor, as if she were going home or to some wonderful, comforting place. There was nothing comforting or wonderful about a hospital, but Sarah knew John was waiting for her at the end of the walk, and so her home was momentarily trapped within this building. She hoped he was doing better today, that his eyes would open and look upon her once more. It was the only thing she wanted right now, and she would give anything to see his face alight with happiness and life again.

"Sarah!"

Sarah snapped out of her train of thoughts and glanced down the hall to see Jessica hurrying towards her, a smile plastered upon her face. Sarah felt her heart instantly speed up, a dash of hope sprinkling upon it. "What is it?" she quickly asked.

Jessica took her hand and started leading down the hall. "I have good news. John finally came to his senses. He has improved greatly since yesterday. He even asked about you!" Sarah felt a little lightheaded, and could barely do more than smile. "The doctor said it will be about a week or so before he starts feeling like himself again, but he's out of danger now."

William was standing outside of John's door, but Sarah barely noticed him as Jessica pulled her there. John was recovering; he was feeling better—not entirely like himself but well enough to ask questions and recognize people.

"I've already spoken to him," continued Jessica in a rush, "so you can go in alone to talk with him for a while.

He must be waiting to see you—to make sure you're all right with his own eyes."

Sarah nodded, still dazed, and was about to go into the room when William spoke.

"It seems like everything's fine," he said. "So I'll be heading home. Call me if you need anything. I'll see you tomorrow."

"Sure, sure," murmured Sarah, anxious to get into the room now. "Thanks, Bill."

"It's no trouble," said William, pulling on his coat.

"Take care of yourself."

Sarah nodded quickly and then bolted towards the door. She turned the handle and ventured inside. John was lying in bed, his face still, though his chest moved up and down. He was sleeping, the chaos of the world outside nonexistent in his mind, and Sarah moved to the bedside to stand next to him.

There were bruises on his face, hands, and arms, and the cords were still hooked into his wrist and nose, but he was alive and going to recover. Sarah felt tears in her eyes and she wiped them quickly away. A smile broke over her face and she laughed quietly. Her prayers had been answered; her faith in John and her own strength had been enough to overcome this terrible ordeal.

She lifted his hand and gently kissed it. Suddenly his eyes fluttered open and his gaze fell upon her. Sarah's breath caught in her throat and she closed her mouth, feeling speechless. She could see into his eyes again, could feel the warmth of his hand in hers. It was too perfect, too wonderful. A tear slid down her cheek and splashed upon his hand. John looked down towards it and then back to Sarah, a smile slowly tracing his lips.

"John ..." whispered Sarah. She bent forward and softly kissed his forehead, brushing away hair that hung

in her way. She held his hand firmly and sat on the

bed, trying to remain as close as possible to her love. She had to remind herself that this moment was real. It wasn't a dream or her imagination conjuring these images up. It was real, and John was okay.

"Sarah, I want to spend the rest of my life with you," said John softly. His thumb touched the ring upon her finger. "I want your life and mine to be intertwined."

"Yes," said Sarah, almost laughing again from happiness. "We'll live this life together—a life of love —our love."

John's eyes grew troubled and they shifted to the bed. "But ... I'm afraid of dying. I'm not ready to take that road yet."

Sarah quickly leaned forward and pressed her lips against his, kissing him. "Hush, love," she spoke quietly, her voice breaking. "Please don't speak that word again. You'll be all right, and you can never leave me alone."

John looked up from the bed and to Sarah, his smile returning. He gripped her hand tightly and breathed out slowly in relief. Sarah shared his gaze, her eyes glassy. It was all she had wanted—John to be all right—and she had gotten it.

"Sarah? John?"

Both turned to look at the open doorway, and Sarah stood up in surprise as she saw Amanda and

Michael come into the room. There was a wide smile plastered across John's face and he lifted his hand a little to wave.

"Hi!" Amanda was the first to come rushing into the room. She hugged Sarah. "I'm so glad you're both okay!"

"How did you know we were here?" wondered Sarah aloud. During all the despair and misery, Sarah had completely forgotten to call Amanda or Michael —both of which had probably wanted to drop by and visit them.

"Jessica told me over the phone," explained Michael. "It's a horrible accident. I saw it on the news yesterday but you never think it's about someone you know. But man ..." Michael shook his head and looked to John. "I was so worried."

"By the way, my parents are also here to see you," said Amanda.

Sarah started. "Really? Where are they?"

Amanda left the room for a moment and re-entered with Jessica, Caroline and David. The latter of the four walked over to the bed where Sarah stood.

"Hello, young man," he said to John. "How are you feeling now?"

"Much better, thank you," replied John.

Caroline smiled. "I hope you get well soon, John."

"Thanks," he said.

Caroline moved towards her niece and embraced her into a warm hug. She moved away and placed both hands upon her face, studying her. "I was so afraid when I heard the news. Thank God you're all right."

"He answered our prayers," said Jessica softly, folding her hands over her chest. "He gave us a gift of happiness in our time of need."

"And as soon as he recovers we can start planning the wedding," said Amanda brightly. She looked to Sarah and winked. "What do you think?"

"Well, honestly the wedding is the furthest thing from my mind right now," confessed Sarah. "I'm not even thinking about it until John gets out of here."

"You're absolutely right, Sarah," said Michael. "Stop pestering her, Amanda." His wife scowled and crossed her arms. He laughed and looked to John. "Anyway, it's getting late, so we should probably get going. We just dropped by to say hello and wish you a speedy recovery."

"Okay," said John, a little disappointed. "What about Mr. Graham's project?"

Michael waved his hand in the air. "Don't even think about it. I'll finish the project and you just worry about getting better. Understood?"

John grinned. "Got it."

Sarah turned to David. "Uncle, will you go back to

Montclair today?"

"No, my child," he replied. "We'll be staying at Amanda's house for a few days. We'll visit you again tomorrow."

"We bless you, John," said Caroline.

"Thank you," said John, offering another wave as the pair left the room, followed shortly after by Amanda and Michael.

Sarah returned to her position on the bed and Jessica also left, wanting to return home to get some sleep. She had been at the hospital all day so Sarah gave her a hug goodbye and stayed with John, talking with him for a while until he grew tired and shut his eyes.

Sarah felt the tug of sleep also, and when she lay down on the couch in the room, she felt for the first time in days wanting sleep. Her eyes closed and her breathing relaxed. She curled up and drifted off.

❋ ❋ ❋

A noise awoke Sarah. It wasn't a car or an alarm or any of the various hospital noises. The noise was coming

from John. He was moaning in his sleep, crying out like a child, and a terrified expression was upon his face. Sarah jumped up from the couch, completely awake now, and the nurse who had been sitting in the corner with a newspaper also approached the bedside.

"No ... no ... don't touch me!" cried John loudly.

Sarah jumped in surprise at the volume of his voice and glanced quickly up at the nurse, who just shook her head. *Bad dream, then*, thought Sarah in relief. "John, wake up John," she said gently, shaking his shoulder. "You're dreaming. Open your eyes."

John's eyes sprang open and he tried to sit up, but Sarah calmed him, keeping hands on his arms. He slowly allowed himself to lie back down. "Sarah ... oh, Sarah ... I was lost in darkness. My nightmare was ... it was trying to kill me ..."

"No, John," said Sarah slowly, calmly, trying to control her own fear. "I am here beside you. Your nightmares aren't real. They can't hurt you ... John?"

His eyes had closed again and Sarah shook him, a little more forcefully this time. She looked back to the nurse, who quickly checked his pulse and then ran quickly from the room. Sarah's heart was beating madly and she shook him again, crying now.

"John! John, wake up!" she cried, her fingernails digging into his arms.

A doctor appeared in the doorway and motioned for Sarah to step aside. He touched John's wrist and then used his stethoscope to listen to his heart. Another glance was given to the heart rate machine in the corner and finally the doctor turned to Sarah.

"I'm sorry," he said gently.

"Sorry?" echoed Sarah, her legs trembling. "What does that mean? What does 'sorry' mean?"

The doctor placed his stethoscope back around his neck. "It means he is dead."

The world tilted under Sarah's feet and she fell, plummeting into darkness.

✻ ✻ ✻

The church that Sarah so adored a few days before was now a place she despised. A crowd of relatives and friends of John had gathered in the church, filling the seats before the altar. Sarah stared ahead, a throbbing pain at the side of her head. She had fainted at the hospital after hearing those words … the words that still haunted her … and had bumped her head against the floor. It hardly mattered now, though. What was a single pain compared to the death of her beloved?

The sea of black suddenly turned and Sarah gritted her teeth, not wanting to do the same, but she gave it, allowing her eyes to fall upon the procession. It was led by the priest, and two men were by his side carrying a cross and a banner. Michael was one of the pallbearers, a blank look etched upon his face.

Sarah couldn't bear to look any longer. She had been hearing things about the funeral for the past few days: which coffin to buy, where to hold it, who was going, etc, etc. She was sick of it all. She just wanted it to be over so she could mourn in peace.

The casket was placed at the front of the church and now Sarah couldn't look away from it. The priest was speaking, but she tuned his voice out. Her eyes were on

the candles being placed upon the casket. They were being arranged in the shape of a cross.

She looked away.

✸ ✸ ✸

The procession headed to the cemetery, and Sarah followed behind, her arm linked with Jessica's, who was sobbing quietly into a handkerchief. Sarah's tears had since long dried up. Now she was simply hollow inside, no more space left for grief or despair. She was empty, incomplete. Nothing would fill this hole.

The coffin lowered into the ground, and the priest began the traditional funeral speech. Jessica's crying grew louder and Sarah held her close, her eyes fixed upon the casket as it made its way down into the deep earth. That's where her John was going: down into the earth.

William, Michael, Amanda and her parents were all standing behind them, and Sarah felt William's hand upon her shoulder, squeezing it. She didn't have the energy to smile or show any form of gratitude, and the gesture was about as hollow as her heart right now, for she felt nothing.

John had wanted to spend his entire life by her side, to love her, to hold her, to be with her forever. Now everything had changed. Sarah had devoted her life to being with him, to loving him, and now he was gone. What purpose did her life now hold? What more was there for her? She could go back to work, carry on with her life, but it would be a hollow life, a life without love.

How could she possibly do that?

The casket reached the end of the trip into the darkness, and Sarah shut her eyes.

CHAPTER 17

After the funeral, Sarah invited her family over to her home. She stood in the doorway of the living room while Michael, Amanda, and her aunt and uncle sat on the couch. There was only silence between them. That was fine to Sarah. She didn't want to talk about John anyway; it would only bring up painful memories. He was so close to her, even after death, and she didn't want to cry anymore. Crying wouldn't bring John back; crying wouldn't heal her broken heart. Her eyes had gone sore from weeping so much over the past few days, and she was afraid the physical chore of crying would hurt more than the pain itself.

"It was so unexpected," said David softly, shaking his head in disbelief. He was the first to break the awful silence. "I thought he would get well soon."

His wife nodded in agreement but said nothing. She was busy studying her niece, a worried look upon her face. Sarah knew they were all equally worried, but her aunt displayed feelings more easily than the others.

Michael had his face in his hands and was leaned

forward on the couch. "I knew John since our time in university. He was always so transparent. There was never a secret between us." He gave a sad laugh and then turned it into a sigh, rubbing his hands over his eyes. "He wasn't just a business partner. He was a true friend."

"He seemed like a decent young man," agreed David, nodding. "He'll always remain in our hearts."

Sarah couldn't bear this talk any longer. She didn't want to hear them talking about John so casually, so she turned from the living room and attempted to flee

towards her bedroom when her aunt Caroline called her to stop.

"Sarah, don't run off on your own," she warned, approaching her niece. Sarah was led back into the living room and onto a chair. "I know this is hard for you, but you have to find the strength to handle the situation in the best way possible."

"Auntie, I don't know what to do," whispered Sarah, cracking under the stress. "I don't know how to live my life without him." She lifted her gaze slowly to the golden cross pendant hanging around her aunt's neck. "I believe in God, and I also believe that He has a reason for everything He does, but I don't understand why He took John away from me." There was a stinging sensation at the corners of her eyes and she rapidly blinked it away. "He wanted to live his life … and I was committed to live it with him. We were going to be married."

"I know, Sarah," said her uncle David, patting her hand comfortingly. "John's sudden death was a shock; you weren't prepared for something like that. But you can't live life without emotion, and you can't live it alone. Life is a giant struggle—you need help getting through it."

"Sorry, Uncle," whispered Sarah, as she shook her head. "I can't imagine anyone in my life except him. He may not be here in body, but he is here in soul." She touched her chest and pressed her hand against it. "I can feel him."

"Sarah ..." Amanda gently rubbed her cousin's back. "Things happen in life that you just can't stop. You don't have to think about the future just yet, but there's going to come a time when you have to move on and start again.

When that time comes, you'll be strong enough to leave everything behind and begin a new life."

Sarah turned her expression sour and wrapped her arms around her middle to comfort herself. "There's no meaning to life without him," she said determinedly.

Amanda sighed angrily. "You've already lived a part of your life without John. You can do it again— and you *will* do it again. I won't hear any talk of not going on without him."

Sarah was stubborn. She didn't want it to be the end; she didn't want her life without John to start. There was nothing good about moving on and leaving things behind. John was dead, and she knew and accepted this, but that didn't mean she was ready to go on without him. How would Amanda feel if Michael suddenly died? She wanted to ask her cousin this—to ask her what she would do without her husband, but the words wouldn't pass through her lips, and she was glad she didn't say it, as it was a horrible thing to say.

They stayed for a few hours, having coffee and lunch, before throwing on their coats and preparing to leave. Sarah stood in the porch with them, her heart hollow and cold, and let them all hug her and wish her condolences.

"I hate to leave you alone but we have to get back to Montclair," said Caroline, the worried look upon her face growing. "I told Amanda to call you every few hours, though, so keep your phone close."

"It's okay, Auntie, really," said Sarah. "I'll be fine."

Caroline touched her cheek and furrowed her brows in distress. "You take care of yourself."

"I will," replied Sarah.

They then left and Sarah shut the door behind them.

She flicked the lock into place and leaned against the door.

There was a sudden loneliness inside of her, a loneliness she had never felt before. She thought she had felt the worst of it when John had been sick, and again at the funeral, but now it was worse. It grew and grew, overtaking her last remaining bit of hope.

Sarah clutched her chest and ran to the bathroom.

The rushing water of the shower drowned out some of the sadness contained within Sarah's heart, but it still wasn't enough. It was still eating her alive inside. How could she possibly go on like this, to live every day feeling this way? It seemed rather impossible to Sarah—to live a life without John, to live a life without love.

She lathered the shampoo up in her hair and vigorously scrubbed her head, though she stopped after a while, allowing her fingers to glide through her dark strands of hair. She took a deep breath and began to rinse her hair, taking her time. The action brought her some relief, and she felt her body slipping away to some relaxing place.

For a moment she forgot about the pain and the funeral and everything associated with her beloved, but when she stepped out of the shower and into her bedroom, Sarah saw a picture of John on her desk and the pain came rushing back. Against her better judgement, Sarah wandered over to the picture frame and plucked it off the desk and held it within two hands, staring grimly down at it.

It was a photo of her and John at the park flying kites. She recalled the memory fondly. It had been a warm summer's day and they had brought a picnic along with the kites. The wind kept blowing away their paper plates and they would have to chase down the blown away objects before being accused of littering. They had laughed for hours that day, finally leaving when the sun had gone down and returning to Sarah's place to finish their uneaten picnic.

Sarah clumsily placed the photograph back on the desk, nearly knocking over several more in the process. They were nearly all pictures of her and John, a few being occupied by Amanda, her aunt and uncle, and William, along with a few pictures from work. She had brought the ones with John in them to the front, and now they all stood out like a horrible taunt, reminding her that he was no longer in this world.

Sarah fought against crying once more and started to get dressed.

Amanda switched off the last remaining lamp in the bedroom and got into bed, pulling the covers up over herself. Michael was already in bed, a distraught look upon his face. She knew he was hurting inside over the death of his friend. She had not known John very well, but she knew he had been a good person and he had treated her cousin well. She wished there was something she could do to cheer her husband up —perhaps distract him from his horrid thoughts.

His shirt was still on, and Amanda leaned over Michael, trailing her fingers up his chest. She slowly undid the buttons one by one, letting the shirt fall away.

Her hand ran along his stomach and up his chest to his neck, where she kissed him softly.

He didn't seem to notice her there, and Amanda grew more worried. She drew herself farther up and kissed him on the lips, letting the kisses become deep. Still nothing.

Michael then turned away from his wife, allowing his back to face her. Amanda gave a quiet sigh and lay down, troubled by his behaviour. Both he and Sarah were acting the same way, and that worried Amanda. She needed them to be strong, to face this terrible trial of life and get through it. She wished there was something more she could do, but perhaps they just needed time.

The stairs of John's apartment loomed before her, and Sarah clutched her bag tightly, dreading going up there. There were many memories contained in this place, and she knew she was only risking hurting herself, but she wanted to come here. On those stairs she had kissed John in the rain; on those stairs she had walked to meet his mother for the first time. She was meeting her again now.

Jessica was luckily home and opened the door for Sarah. She gave her a hug and welcomed her inside.

"How are you, Sarah?" she asked, her voice drained.

"I'm okay," answered Sarah. "What about you?" She studied Jessica's face for a few seconds and saw the distress clouding her normally happy features. There had been something about her voice, too, a certain hollowness that Sarah knew well. "You haven't been eating or sleeping well, have you?"

"No, I'm fine," replied Jessica, though her eyes diverted from Sarah's.

"That isn't true," said Sarah firmly, placing her bag on the kitchen table. "I can tell you're lying."

Jessica folded her hands together and tucked in her lower lip. "May I ask something of you, Sarah?" Sarah nodded. "Can you stay here with me for a few days? I ... I miss John so much, and I see him in you. If you stay here, it will feel like he is here, as well."

Sarah gazed at Jessica for a long while. "You're a strong woman," she finally said. "You've lost so much ... your husband, your son ... and still you go on with life." She nodded and held her hand out to Jessica. "I will stay here with you. I lost my mother, father, and now my love. I don't want to be alone, so I'll stay here with my memories of John."

"No, Sarah ..." Jessica gripped her hand tightly. "You're young with a full life ahead of you. You can't waste your life thinking about the past." She looked to Sarah's bag and then back again. "I think ... your friend, William, loves you ... but he can't express it."

Sarah started. She let go of Jessica's hand. *William ... loves me?* She had never thought about it before. He had always been a good friend to her, but perhaps ...

"Are you sure?" asked Sarah, her voice low. "We're such good friends ... nothing more."

"I could see it in his eyes," said Jessica, smiling sadly. "I saw what he couldn't reveal to you."

"Jessica ..." Sarah wasn't sure what to say. Was the other woman suggesting that she just forget about John like he was nothing and move on? "William and I are friends, and I don't want to think about another man like that." She wanted to say that maybe someday she would

love again, but the words didn't sound right on her tongue.

"Well, you just keep it in mind." Jessica sat to the table. "When will you stay here?"

"After this weekend," replied Sarah.

Jessica opened her mouth to speak again, but the doorbell interrupted her. Sarah left her place by the table and walked over to the door to open it, allowing Jessica to remain seated. She was surprised to see Michael standing on the other side, and she gave him a wide smile, also pleased to see him. He was dressed in a suit and had a briefcase in hand, which probably meant he had just left work.

"How are you doing, Sarah?" he asked, a mixture of a frown and a smile upon his face. "I'm glad to see you here."

"I am fine," replied Sarah, moving aside so he could come in. They both headed towards the kitchen where Jessica waited. "How is everything going?"

"I keep thinking about John," admitted Michael, placing his briefcase on the table. "I have trouble sleeping. Amanda's trying to help, but …" He shook his head, his words trailing off.

"We feel the same way," said Jessica. She looked to the case on the table. "Did you come for a visit or is there something important you'd like to talk about?"

Michael opened up the case and began talking out papers. "I came for business, I'm afraid. I'd like to transfer all of John's shares to your name. I have the paperwork completed. You just have to sign your name."

Jessica stared blankly at the papers as they were laid out in front of her. She looked up to Michael. "I have no interest in business," she admitted quietly, "and I don't

want to get involved in anything at this age." She motioned to Sarah. "You should transfer them to Sarah's name. She has her whole life ahead of her, and I believe she will be the right person to handle John's shares and fulfill any dreams he may have had."

Sarah looked from Jessica to Michael and back again. "No," she said, shaking her head. "No, I can't." *The shares should go to Jessica*, she thought. *She's his mother. She deserves to have them.*

"Sarah ... I think Jessica is right about this," said Michael. "I think you're the right person to have them, and I think John would agree if he were here. You don't have to worry about anything—I'll handle it after you sign the papers. I won't even bother you again about it."

Sarah slowly nodded and sat down. Michael slid the papers towards her and fished a pen out of his pocket. She then began reading through the documents and signed her name each time she was prompted to do so. When everything was finished, Michael took the papers back and returned them to his briefcase.

CHAPTER 18

The days had been going by so slowly for Sarah after John's death. She didn't know what day it was or what time or even if it were day or night sometimes. She knew that tomorrow she was moving in with Jessica, however, and that brought her some kind of happiness. She knew she would be reminded of John while living at his mother's apartment, but she felt being there would also be good for her. If she could grow strong enough to face the house her passed beloved once lived in, she could do anything.

Right now William was giving her a ride home ... a ride to an empty house that contained memories of a person that no longer existed. Sarah gritted her teeth and stared out the window. She promised herself that she wouldn't cry again, but it was getting harder and harder after each passing day. John was constantly in her thoughts, constantly at her home and wherever she went. is face was always present; he was always beside her.

But I can't touch or hear you, thought Sarah, and her lip began to quiver. *No, stop it. No crying, remember?*

Her brain didn't seem to want to listen to her any longer. She felt her eyes overflow and tears began falling down her cheeks, staining the blush she had applied earlier.

"Sarah?" William was looking at her in distress and she tried to smile back, but only a frown seemed to want to show itself. William pulled the car over, surprising Sarah, and turned it off.

"It's okay—I'm okay," said Sarah, attempting to lift her hand to wipe away the tears. She was shocked when

William took her hand and put it aside. He pulled a tissue from his pocket and gently cleaned the tears from her cheeks before returning his attention back to the car.

It roared to life and they were driving again.

Sarah simply gazed at him through the corner of her eye for the remainder of the trip. Jessica's words came rushing back to her mind. She had said that William loved her, and although she had been doubtful before, she was now confident that what Jessica said was indeed true.

It made her a little nervous to think about.

✻ ✻ ✻

The drive had been quiet from that point on, and William walked Sarah to her door when they arrived at her house. Sarah wasn't really sure what to expect after the scene in the car, but her suspicions grew when she felt William's hand slip gently into her own from behind. She slowly turned around to face him.

He was very close to her, closer than he had ever been. Sarah could see the light specks in his dark eyes, and she realized that he was a handsome man. She had perhaps always known this, but he had always been like a friend to her so it didn't matter.

"Sarah ..." William gazed intently into her eyes, a look of longing upon his face. There was love in his eyes, and that was very clear to her now. "Sarah, I know I shouldn't be saying this right now ... but I can't just pretend I don't feel this way. I can't go on without saying something." He paused and took a breath. "I love you, Sarah. I always have."

Sarah was silent. She didn't know what to say to that. She supposed it was the words any woman would want to hear, but they were not words she wanted to hear, and then Jessica's voice came back to her once more, telling her that she couldn't live this life alone, that she had to find someone to share it with.

William began to lean towards her, and Sarah stayed rooted to her spot on the porch. Maybe if he kissed her ... maybe then she would feel something and begin the life everyone wanted her to begin: a life that could be shared with someone.

But when his lips were about to touch hers, when she could feel his warm breath upon her skin, Sarah stepped back, a little dazed, and hurried inside, shutting the door behind her. Her heart was pounding and her legs felt weak. She stumbled towards the bedroom and fell upon her bed, crying wildly into her soft pillows.

What was wrong with her? Jessica was right about William: he was a good man. Why shouldn't she love him? He was decent, handsome, a good friend and always there when she needed him.

Sarah gazed miserably at the picture on her nightstand and reached over to grab it. John's face stared back at her through the glass and she hugged it to her chest.

It's because of you, she thought. *I'm still in love with you, even though you're gone, and I can't imagine another man in my life. William is just a friend—a good friend—but that's all he is to me. How can I just change that when it's you I love and will always love? That's what I believe in: one life, one love. And I simply love you.*

Sarah kissed the picture frame and returned it to the nightstand.

The tiny screen was blank, and Sarah eyed it anxiously, awaiting a sign to appear. For days now she had been feeling sick, throwing up during the early hours of the morning and unable to eat much afterwards. She hadn't thought about pregnancy until the last moment, and now she had finally gone to the super market and purchased a home pregnancy kit. The test was held within her hands, and she wasn't sure what to expect from it. She may have been imagining the entire thing, but a thorough check had to be done.

Suddenly, the screen wasn't blank anymore. A positive sign appeared.

Sarah stared at it impassively for a few minutes, allowing the news to sink in. She then placed it upon her desk and turned towards the full-length mirror in her bedroom. She lifted up her shirt and turned sideways, studying her stomach.

"Oh my God ..." she murmured, breaking into a smile. There was a small bump there. "I'm pregnant!"

She took a deep breath and looked towards John's picture on the desk. *Thank you, John,* she silently said, tears of joy in her eyes. *I now have a reason to live my life in happiness.*

She pushed down her shirt and began gathering the rest of her things. A new journey was about to start and she had to be prepared for it.

Her luggage was heavy, but that didn't stop

Sarah from hauling it all up the stairway
to Jessica's apartment at once. She knocked
on the door and waited for Jessica to

open it, a huge smile plastered across her face. Jessica
shared this smile, unknowing what Sarah knew
for the time being. Sarah pushed her bags into the
apartment and turned to face the older woman.

"I'm glad you decided to stay with me," said Jessica
excitedly, and she was mildly surprised when Sarah
took her hands and led her towards the living room to
sit upon the couch.

"I have good news for you," said Sarah eagerly,
unable to keep the information locked away inside of
her any longer.

Jessica was curious now, and Sarah knew she was
probably thinking upon the few things that could
possibly be good in their sad time. John had died only a
little while ago, so good news was hard to find. "What
is it, Sarah?"

Sarah suddenly became very shy. "I'm pregnant,"
she said quietly.

Jessica blinked in surprise and slowly opened her
mouth, a little speechless. "What?" was all she said.

"I'm pregnant," repeated Sarah, smiling again
now. The excitement of having a purpose to life was
overwhelming. "I was feeling sick all week and so I
tested myself today. It was positive! I'm having John's

baby!"

Jessica's face turned from surprised to worried. "But Sarah ... you aren't married ... and you're so young." She took her hand, concern coating her expression. "I just want you to say that you won't waste your life—that you won't give up your job and hobbies and everything important to you."

"Waste my life?" Sarah took her hand out of Jessica's. "I am having this child. I don't really have any

other choice, do I? Should I abort my child just because of what others might say or think?" She shook her head firmly. "I can't do that—I won't. Our life together has just begun."

Jessica frowned. "I am not telling you to abort your child. In fact, I'm glad that you have chosen to give birth to my grandchild. But others in your position might not feel the same way—and for good reason. Being a single mother is a terrible struggle. I know firsthand how hard it can be."

"And that's why you are my inspiration," said Sarah. "I saw the man John grew into, and I know that you did an excellent job raising him. So I know that with your help, my baby can grow into that same kind of person. There are many single mothers in the world. I'm not the first to live my life only for my baby." She sighed. "That's all I want. It's all I need."

❋ ❋ ❋

A few days had passed since Sarah discovered the fantastic and hope inspiring news. She was at work, sitting at her desk in her office and humming away when she heard a knock on the door. It was slightly open and when she looked up she saw William standing just outside. There was a strange look upon his face.

"May I come in, Sarah?" he asked, his voice a little off.

"Y-yeah, come in," replied Sarah, nodding. She hadn't spoken to William since he tried to kiss her the other night, and she was a little nervous about what he had to say about it.

William entered the room and closed the door behind him. He took a seat in front of the desk. "Listen, Sarah," he began, a little remorsefully, "I feel extremely sorry for everything I did and said the other night. It was selfish of me, and I put our friendship in jeopardy."

Sarah held up her hand and shook her head. "No, it's all right, Bill," she said.

He glanced up at her in surprise. "It is?" he asked.

"Well ..." Sarah bit her lip, not really sure how to explain herself. It wasn't *that* all right, but she understood love and what it did to people. "I'm not going to condemn you for speaking your feelings. I'm just sorry I couldn't return them."

William nodded, a little disappointed. "It's okay. I just want to be a part of your life," he said quietly.

Sarah gave a soft smile. "You are a part of my life, Bill," she responded.

He returned the smile and nodded again. He rose from the chair. "Remember, I'll always be here if you need me."

"I know," said Sarah.

* * *

The park was beautiful today, and Sarah strolled along the edge of the glimmering lake, watching other people as they ran about doing various activities. It had been a few months since she first found out she was pregnant, and she could feel the baby move occasionally inside of her. Only a few months more and she would welcome a new life into this world, a life that was shared between her and John. She wished sometimes that he could be here to witness the birth of his child, that he was

alive and would watch his child grow up to become an adult, but that kind of thinking always made her sad.

Sarah approached a part of the lake that was familiar to her, a part that was filled with memories, and stood at its edge with closed eyes. She breathed in the warm air.

I can feel you John... I know you would be watching

over me all through this journey called life... whenever I look next to me, I feel like you are here... and a part of you is within me in the form of this child... Love is like the wind... you may not see it... especially in the absence of the other... but you always feel it around... She smiled as the warm sun graced her face. *I love you so much. Our love is eternal.*

Sarah opened her eyes again and looked down to her boots. Pebbles were scattered everywhere. She picked up a handful and faced the lake.

John had once shown her how to skip rocks here, and she was confident that she could now do it. She remembered that day so clearly, as if it had happened yesterday.

Sarah lifted her hand and threw the first rock. It bounced effortlessly across the surface of the water, and she laughed aloud.

"Life has finally come full circle!" she cried, and laughed again.

After waiting the remaining months of her pregnancy, Sarah soon found herself rushed to the hospital one afternoon by Jessica. It had been a quick birthing, and afterwards Sarah lay in bed, exhausted and gazing tiredly at the ceiling.

Crying filled the room and Sarah leaned up on her pillows. Jessica was standing nearby with a blue bundle cradled in her arms. It moved in her grasp and Sarah reached out her arms to take it.

"He looks exactly like John did when he was born," said Jessica with a smile as she passed the baby to Sarah.

My baby, Sarah thought giddily, as she supported the infant in her arms. She tickled his chin with her finger and smiled down at him, tears leaking from the corners of her eyes. She could feel John in the room with her, also gazing at their child with affection.

Sarah knew that he was watching them—that he would always watch over them.

ACKNOWLEDGEMENT

My love and thanks to my parents, siblings/cousins, relatives and friends. "Thank you all for supporting me".

I would like to thank also my development editors, especially Sandra Harvey and Aishwarya Sivakumar for their contributions and efforts.

I also appreciate the readers of this book and I hope they will enjoy this book.

Finally, thanks to all reviewers of this book for their comments, suggestions, and recommendations.

ABOUT THE AUTHOR

Santonu Kumar Dhar is an entrepreneur and novelist. He was born on 28 March, 1986 to a Bengali Hindu family in Cumilla, Bangladesh. Ratan Ranjan Dhar, his father, is a businessman, while Mita, his mother, is a housewife. He holds a Level 7 qualification of Chartered Management Institute (CMI), UK and has been a Fellow of the institute since October 2018. He had a desire of creating stories that readers would fall in love with since he was a child, but he had to put his dream on hold in order to focus on his studies and job. Finally, in 2012, he was able to put pen to paper with the publication of his first novel, Life Of Love, which was originally published in 2013. He writes novels with themes that include love, tragedy and fate.

www.ingramcontent.com/pod-product-compliance
Lightning Source LLC
Chambersburg PA
CBHW020639260626
47157CB00008B/2817